Praise for Peter Benson's Previous Novels

The Levels

A delight – a funny, painful, beautiful book – *Jane Gardam*

Benson's strong visual sense conjures up vivid imagery from the heart of the countryside. – *Sunday Times*

A very apt and unillusioned sort of modern pastoral, blessed with the kind of narrative gift that's like perfect pitch. – *The Guardian*

A Lesser Dependency

The lack of adornment lends the novel the directness of a folk tale and sharpens its sting. – *The Independent*

...touched with poetry. Benson's gift is to capture in strong visual terms the earth-based intuition of those 'dropped in the sand and tuned to the rhythms of tiny island life'. – *Sunday Times*

The Shape of Clouds

Vividly, defiantly realistic at times, luridly surreal at others, his writing's ability to compound striking meteaphors of the abstract with a graphic physicality has won him a deserved following. – *TLS*

Beautiful writing and thoughtful language... page after page of stunning prose. – *Time Out*

D11157650

The Other Occupant

Restrained, deadpan and unaffected, Peter Benson has one of the most distinctive voices in modern British fiction... a gem of understatement and compassion. – *Evening Standard*

Layers and crevices, gaps and fissures as important as what is said, all add up to a short novel of power and persuasiveness. – *Financial Times*

A rare book: compact, exquisitely crafted and intensely upsetting... Benson's cryptic, understated style is ideally suited to the emotive themes which he develops. – *Sunday Times*

Two Cows and a Vanful of Smoke

One of the most distinctive voices in modern British fiction – *Evening Standard*

The real magic of the book is in its evocation of a mystical English countryside... the prose twists and rolls like a vine creeping over a medieval brick wall. – *New Statesman*

An adventure story written in Benson's distinctive, flourished-filled style and suffused with his deep and abiding love of the West Country. – *Daily Mail*

THE STROMNESS DINNER

Although this story is based on things that happened, it is a novel. This means that in Orkney a lake is known as a loch, for example.

THE STROMNESS DINNER

PETER BENSON

SEREN

Seren is the book imprint of
Poetry Wales Press Ltd,
Suite 6, 4 Derwen Road, Bridgend, Wales, CF31 1LH

www.serenbooks.com
facebook.com/SerenBooks
Twitter: @SerenBooks

This is a work of fiction. All of the characters, organisations, and events
portrayed in this novel are either products of the author's imagination or
are used ficticiously.

ISBN: 9781781725962
Ebook: 9781781725979

A CIP record for this title is available from the British Library.

The publisher acknowledges the financial assistance
of the Welsh Books Council.

Cover image by Eilidh Warnock
https://eilidhwarnock.wixsite.com/mysite/

Printed by Bell & Bain, Glasgow.

ONE

WE WERE BEECH BUILDING SERVICES

My dad and I were Beech Building Services. We did all kinds of work. No job too small. You called us. You told us what you needed. We'd turn up with a tape measure and a pencil. We'd give you a quote. If you liked the quote, we'd do the job. If the quote didn't suit, we'd leave you alone. We were easy. We were Beech Building Services. We were based in Bermondsey, which is an area of London.

Dad used to live in Margate, which is by the sea. When he was younger he used to come up to the city for weekends and spend time with his Auntie Carol who lived on Tower Bridge Road. One weekend he met Mum in a pub. They got on. When the weekend was over, he went home but promised her he'd be back. He kept his promise. He went back. He bought a ring. She said yes. He went great. They got married. He decided he didn't want to go back to Margate so they rented a place on Crosby Row. They had me. Later, he bought a place on Crosby Row, and later, after he'd got going with the building and decorating, he rented a lock-up to keep materials and the bigger tools, and the mixer. Then they had Sally. Beech Building Services was a small firm, but we didn't want to be any bigger. We were good as we were.

We did plastering, joinery, roofs and decorating. If we needed a plumber we used Bob from Eland Plumbing & Heating. If we needed a sparks we used P.G. Electrics. We had 17 reviews on checkatrade.com with an average score of 9.87. At Beech Building Services we were proud of the service we offered.

We were busy. In 2018 we worked on twenty five big jobs and a couple of dozen weekenders. We liked to work.

My dad is Jack. He's big and bald. Have a look at his gut. Check his neck. He likes his food. I'm Ed. I like my food, but in a different way to the way Dad likes it. He likes it because it tastes good and fills him up. I like it because I like to think about it, read about it, cook it and eat it. I should also say that I'm bigger than Dad. People can see me coming. I don't lumber in but I can be useful. I don't work out but I keep fit. That's being a builder for you. I stay around fourteen and a half stone. It's a healthy weight for my size. When I was at school I was called "Oi" but only once.

I like food and I like being neat. I kept my room neat, I kept the lock-up neat, I kept my clothes neat. Okay so when I was working I had to wear overalls and they got to look crap after a while, and my boots were knackered, but everyone has to make exceptions. Dad sometimes said my neatness was annoying but I told him being neat made us a better team, and customers liked it. They liked it when a job was half done and they came home and their homes were tidy, and I did too.

My mum is Joyce and a hairdresser. She goes to old peoples' homes and care centres and does the residents' hair. She likes food but I don't know where she puts it. She's a bit round in places, but otherwise I don't think her doctor would tell her to cut down on butter. My sister is Sally. She's a nurse. She likes her work. It keeps her fit. Boys will like her but they don't know her and she won't tell them. They have to find out for themselves. The dog's Barney. He looks like he couldn't hurt a fly, but if we were on a job and he was guarding the van, you wouldn't want to try and nick some tools. He'd have your hand for a snack and your balls for afters. He's the most philosophical dog in Bermondsey. Every-one loves Barney. He loves food.

Have a word with my Mum. Even I can tell why you would. Have the wrong word with her, or try something tasty, and she'll boil your toes. And if you're feeling brave, have another word with Sally. Sally is gorgeous. Cross her and she will do you up.

So there you have us.

We are the Beech family.

Get in.

We would do your job.

I WAS PARKED AND MET MARCUS BOWEN

Dad and I had a van. We had it sign written. It said "BEECH BUILD-ING SERVICES. DECORATING. KITCHENS. EXTENSIONS." on the side. Below that it had our number and an email address. We didn't have a website but we'd thought about it. We'd put boxes in the local freebie and online but the van was the best ad. If you parked it outside a job you'd get a call or a note under the wiper.

So we were doing a job on Page's Walk. It was tiling a kitchen, fitting new tops and doors, sorting the floor and doing other stuff. It was a usual Tuesday in May. It was warm, just right. I went down to the van to eat a doughnut and fetch a drill. As I was sort-ing out the bits, an Audi TT pulled up behind me and a bloke in a suit got out. I say "suit" but this wasn't any old suit. This was fitted and sharp, blue so dark it was almost black, matched with a pressed shirt and a shiny tie with embroidered flowers on it. His hair was dark and floppy, and his shave was tight. Polished brogues. Class.

"Hi," he said.

"Hi yourself," I said.

"I've just moved in over there." He pointed over his shoulder. "The Jam Factory."

"Nice," I said.

"It is. You do kitchens?"

"Doing one now."

"Excellent. So could you give me a quote? I'll want new work-tops, cupboards, bits and pieces."

"We could do that."

He fished for his wallet, pulled out a card and gave it to me. "I'm in tomorrow night. Half seven okay?"

"Sure." I looked at the card. His name was Marcus Bowen. He worked for a firm in the City. The card said he was a Consultant Strategist. I was going to ask what that was but then I didn't. It didn't matter. I like people who get straight to the point. He might have been posh but I could tell he was sound. I said "See you then, Marcus…" instead.

"And you're?"

"Ed."

"Thanks Ed," and he got back in his car and drove off.

I sorted the drill and the rest of the bits, gave Barney some biscuits and made sure he had enough water, and went "Grrr…" at him. He growled at me and ate one of the biscuits. He's better than any alarm you could buy. He'd have your hand for a snack and your balls for afters. I've already told you this, but it's worth repeating. Barney. He's a philosopher.

So I went upstairs to this flat. It was okay. Dad was in the kitchen. It was knackered. We'd done most of the prep but needed to sort a couple of damp patches. I said "Here you go," and put the drill and the rest of the bits on the worktop.

"Ta," he said.

"Cuppa?" I said.

"Why not?"

I put the kettle on and as I fished for some tea bags and milk and sugar and mugs I told Dad about the bloke I'd met in the street. He nodded and said "You want me there?"

"Up to you."

He picked up the drill and whizzed it once. The batteries were charged. I'd done that. Be prepared. That's what I always think.

He said "Reckon you can handle it?"

"Don't see why not."

"It's yours then."

Giving a quote is simple. We'd got it down. It's not a fine art. I've been to Amsterdam and while I was there I spent at least an hour in an art gallery so I know what I'm talking about.

THE JAM FACTORY
AND LONDON'S LARDER

Bermondsey used to be London's larder. There were factories all over. Baking was big business. The area used to be called biscuit town. The world's first canning factory was in Bermondsey. Then there was brewing and jam making. So when Mr Hartley the jam man from up north wanted to build a factory in London, he came to Bermondsey and ended up building one, then two, then three. They still talk about him because he was a top boss. The workers were paid over the odds, got a share of the profits and a pension, and a doctor was always on call. Mr Hartley organised outings to the coast, dances at the weekends, all sorts. The business went tits up in the 1960s, and although the buildings escaped demolition they got knackered. So when they were done up for flats it was sweet for the old bricks and the area, and the posh lot moved in.

There are people who say that when you get posh moving in the area takes a dive, but that's bollocks. It does nothing of the sort. When I was a kid, the streets of Bermondsey were mental. Okay, so you've got to keep your wits about you now, but nothing like it was in the old days. And when my old man was a kid it was even worse. He was in The Pagoda once, and there were some blokes in there who'd come up looking for the Cuban boxers who trained in the gym on Leroy Street. Useful south paws mostly. So the blokes were brazen about it, telling the landlord they were tooled up and what was he going to do about it and okay he could have dealt with one or two on their own, there was no way he was handling some gang with razored bats. So when the Cubans came round it kicked off and then it was a riot, and there had to be thirty blokes kicking lumps out of each other in the middle of Tower Bridge Road. And that's a busy thoroughfare, and when the police came they got fighting too, and by the end of the night there were people dead outside where the picture framers is now. These days you might get some lad called Harry having a fight with some lad called Timothy because Timothy looked at Harry's girlfriend Amanda, but it's just swinging and missing over some clam linguini and a glass of Chablis and no one's even a useful south paw, and they go home arm in arm. And that's not progress? I call it peace.

So the next night I went round and rang Marcus Bowen's buzzer at half seven on the dot. That's another thing. Start as you mean to go on. Be on time. Get in. He buzzed me up and I was in the lift. I'd not been in The Jam Factory since they did it up and I could tell it was quality. It worked. It was smooth. It smelt of gloss. I got out at the fourth floor and he was waiting for me at his door. "Hi," he said, and I said "All right?"

"Yeah."

"Cool."

I slipped on a pair of disposable overshoes (always a good touch and punters never expect it) and just as well because the flat was immaculate – a two bed with one en-suite, separate bathroom and a lounge/kitchen/diner. There was exposed brickwork and a cast iron column between the kitchen area and the dining table. That was a nice feature. There were some great views towards the city, and the worktops and cupboards looked perfect to me, but he didn't like the style. I could see what he meant. The doors were white and the worktops were 20mm black granite, and he said "I want something more in keeping with the original style of the place. More wood."

"Okay," I said. So there's beech block, oak block..."

"Oak," he said.

"Good choice."

"And oak for the cupboards."

I went to one of the cupboards and opened it. "The carcasses are good. You want to keep them?"

"Carcasses?"

"Yeah. The frame, the back, the shelves. We don't need to replace them – all we do is fit new doors, sides and tops and you're away. Hell of a lot less disruption and you'll save big time."

"Money's not a problem," he said, "but I can see the sense."

"We'll do whatever you want, Mr Bowen..."

"Marcus..."

"Marcus. But if we're going to rip all this out we're talking weeks."

"How long if you've just replacing the tops and doors?"

"A week at most."

"Okay."

"Want me to measure up?"

"Sure," he said, so I did. It took me fifteen minutes. He left me to it. He went to a bedroom to make a phone call. I could hear him talking. I heard him say "You know I do..." and "About half nine."

When I'd done I waited for him to finish and looked at his stuff. He had photographs on the walls, and a framed poster for a place called The Pier Arts Centre. He had books I'd never heard of on light wooden shelves, and a collection of knick-knacks. I say knick-knacks but they weren't the sort of knick-knacks Mum would have at ours. She likes things like glass puppies and birds on branches that look like real birds. Marcus Bowen had stuff that looked valuable. There was an angular sculpture with holes in it that could have been a man, and a copper star mounted in a block of granite. I think this was a miniature weather vane. There was a very carefully carved wooden house on stilts with windows made of pebbles, and a delicately inscribed silver apple. The man had taste, and when he'd finished his call and came from the bedroom, he said "Okay. Got all you need?"

"I think so."

"I'll have to get some prices, but I should have something for you in a couple of days."

"Great."

IN THE MILLER
WITH NURSES

When I left The Jam Factory I went down The Miller, my local. It wasn't the best looking boozer but it did me, my mates Stu and Mo and the doctors and nurses from the hospital next door. That's Guy's. Doctors and nurses like a drink. I'd seen my doctor a couple of weeks earlier because I'd stuck a screwdriver in the back of my hand, and he wanted to check it was healing proper. Once he'd done that he asked me how much I drank. When I told him, he said I should cut down. So when I told him about the doctors and nurses I knew in The Miller, he said "That's as maybe." Then he asked me if I smoked. I told him that I didn't do fags but I sometimes had a toot on the weekends, but only weekends. "Can't be blazed on a working day. Not with the tools we use." He gave me a look over the top of his glasses and then said "Careful as you go." He was a good bloke.

I've been out with a few nurses. One was called Hannah. When we were going out, she was working in the urgent care centre. She dealt with stuff like broken bones and burns and idiots who've stuck screwdrivers into the back of their hands. She had very gentle hands. She was Irish. She smelt of apples and pastry and had skin that looked like full fat milk. We were good together. We weren't jealous which was just as well because she was well into anyone. She shared a flat with a nurse from South Africa called Charity, and one night they got hammered and ended up in bed together. Hannah was honest with me and told me all about it. I was well turned on. I told her that next time it happened she should text and I'd come over. It did and she did and I did, and it was mental. Nurses are the best.

Hannah moved back to Galway. She was born there. She got a job in the hospital. When we said goodbye I was sad but I was glad too because I could see she was happy to being going home, and London had never suited her. She said "Don't miss me, Ed. And you're always welcome to visit, you know that."

"Thanks," I said, and to cheer myself up I went to a top restaurant and had the best dinner ever. The next week I met an Occupational Therapist called Susan. She was the most flexible woman I have ever met. She could tuck her ankles behind her neck. She was from Wolverhampton. She wasn't jealous either. I think it's a nurse thing, this. They see so much dirt and death that they've learnt that nothing is forever, temporary is the state of the world and we spend out lives practising goodbyes. So they can't be troubling themselves with the whats and whys of whether whoever they're with is only with them and them alone. I suppose faithfulness does come to everyone one day, so there's no point forcing it.

At the time when I was in The Miller after seeing Marcus Bowen about his kitchen I was seeing Magda. She was Polish and had been Catholic but had given it up after she found out the priest at her home had been off with choirboys. I told her I thought if God was so clever why are oranges sticky, and she couldn't argue with that. She wasn't a nurse. She worked in a restaurant in The Shard. The Shard is the tallest building in the country. It's amazing. One day I met her there when she came off her shift and we had a couple of drinks. After my second I went to the toilet. The place where you took a piss was a glass wall and beyond that there was the window so it was like you were pissing onto the trains hundreds of metres below.

So I was in The Miller and I'd been to see Marcus Bowen in The Jam Factory. I'd had a word with Jim the landlord, bought a pint, found a seat and texted Magda. She rented a place round the corner. It was her day off. I thumbed "Fancy a pint?" Stupid question. She loved a pint. Ten minutes later she was pushing her way into the pub. She was with her brother who was over from Warsaw to see if he could get a job. He was an engineer called Natan and wanted to work on the underground. I bought a round and we went back to where I was sitting and while Magda texted whoever, I told him that I knew someone who worked at the Neasden depot and I'd give him a call. He said he'd already had an interview at Hainault, and reckoned he'd done all right.

So we were drinking and I was telling Natan about my day and how if the old man and I weren't working on a kitchen then we were working on a kitchen, and he thought this was funny. He said something about loving the British sense of humour. I told him we loved Polish sausage. "There, you see," he said. "So funny." I don't know if he was checking me out, making sure I was okay for his sister, but it didn't matter because we were splitting up anyway. I knew it, she knew, we knew it but we hadn't decided when and how, just definite. Which is probably the best way to go about these things. Just know it's not working and say "See you later" even though both of you know that's the last thing that's happening.

My mum had a word with me about this, said "When Dad and I were your age it was different. We never behaved like you and your sister."

"What you talking about?"

"Once we were courting that was it. There was no going back. It wasn't a game to us."

"I'm talking about Sally."

"What about her?"

"You said 'you and your sister' like Sally's on the game or something."

Mum shook her head. "Typical. One rule for you, another for her."

"Eh?"

"You know what I mean, Ed."

I suppose I did. I suppose I knew she could do what she wanted, and if she wanted to she could do what she wanted, but she was my sister and she was twenty two and if someone took advantage of her they'd have a problem. Yeah I know, she can take care of herself, but I was her brother and if she needed me to have a quiet word, I'd have a quiet word. This wasn't a soap opera, but it could have been.

So I was drinking with Magda and Natan and because he was staying I didn't go back to hers after, and because our place is small I went back to mine on my own. I needed an early night anyway. It had been a busy week and I was knackered.

THE SCAR ON HER FLAWLESS FACE

A couple of days later I went back to The Jam Factory with the quote for Marcus Bowen's kitchen. Once we'd gone through it he said "Looks good to me…" and offered me a beer. I said that I didn't mind if I did and he passed me a bottle. It was exactly the sort I expected. Something from the Czech Republic with a name no one but a Czech person can say. We drank. I can tell a good beer and this was better than good. This was gold with balls.

We were talking start dates and stuff when the buzzer rang. A woman said "It's me." Marcus said "Come on up."

"Thanks."

"I'll have to chuck you out in a minute," he said. "That's my sister, and we've got to talk family."

"Of course," I said.

"But I think Monday next would be fine."

"I'll have to check with my old man, but yeah, good…"

He stood up, patted me on the shoulder and went to the front door, and a moment later came back with his sister. She was a woman who looked like she understood power, money and threads. I expected her to look down her nose at me, but when Marcus said "Ed, this is Claire," she smiled and put out a hand, and as we shook she said "Nice to meet you, Ed," as if it really was. Her voice was posh but not too posh, and she had a faint lisp, and her hand was like crumpled tissue paper in mine. I was embarrassed that something so soft should have to touch something so rough. I said "Hi."

She smiled at me. Her eyes were green and bright. I think she might have used some of those eye drops that are useful when you've been sanding and forgotten your goggles. Her hair was short and neat and brown. She had a tiny scar on her chin. It was the size and shape of a pared finger nail, and a shade lighter than the rest of her skin which was tanned but not too tanned. Not a bed tan. This was a tan from somewhere class and the sort of tan you get when you know how bad the sun can be. Just a touch.

She took off her coat and dropped it on the couch, and as she did the air blossomed with the scent of her perfume. I could try and tell you what the scent was, how it reminded me of a fruit cake without the cake, a bucket of ice without the water, and the back of the Tandoori at the top end of the Tower Bridge Road, but I wouldn't be close. So I'll add that it smelled of a dream though using the word "smelled" sounds wrong, because it really didn't smell at all. It scented or chimed or maybe it hummed – I'm not exactly sure – but it was like a load of notes all played in harmony with each other, and although I tried hard not to stand there with my mouth hanging open like a drooling fool, I could not stop myself. She was wearing one of those suits you know cost five grand, and her blouse was blinding white, and she had little earrings that were circles of blue enamel set in a silver ring. Her watch sparkled and the scar on her chin made her face flawless. And as Marcus went to a cupboard and took out a wine glass, and went to the fridge and pulled out a bottle of wine, I said "Er…" and finished my beer. Then I said "Thanks for the beer, Marcus. Once I've got the materials, I'll give you a call. Should be later this week."

"Ed's doing the kitchen," Marcus said.

"Good for you," Claire said. She crossed her legs. The air in the flat crackled. I opened my mouth to say something but the words were stuck in there like rubbish. I could feel them being crap. I went for the door. Marcus followed me. I could tell he knew. I suppose he'd seen it before. "Okay," he said. I bent down to take off my overshoes. "Yeah," I said, and stepped into the hallway outside the flat. "Laters."

"Of course."

I headed down the hallway and he closed the door. I reached the lift. I pushed the button. I heard it whirr. I looked back towards Marcus's flat. The lift arrived. The doors opened. I stepped inside. The doors closed.

The lift was full of Claire's scent. I stood there for a moment, closed my eyes and let it fill me. I opened my eyes. I looked at the buttons. I didn't care about the buttons. They could have been liquorice allsorts or the eyes of a numbered beast. I was feeling weird. I wasn't used to feeling weird. When I got outside, I stood on the street for a few minutes and took some deep breaths. It wasn't raining.

Twenty minutes later I was in The Miller with a pint. That helped. Magda was working so I didn't call her, but a couple of girls I've known since way back were there, so I went and talked to them. One was called Rachael and the other was called Jo, and they told me that some bloke we all knew from school had been shot in Dalston. I said "Dalston?" and they said "Yeah…" and I said "What was he doing up there?" and they said "Dunno." I went to Dalston once, but going up there was like going to the moon. It was like "why?"

Rachael and I had something way back, but she'd gone solid muff so we were cool and both knew it. I think Jo didn't give a toss either way but whatever, I thought, because all I could smell was Claire's perfume, that long scent of flowers and spices and cake without the cake and ice and a dropped, beautiful coat, and that lift in The Jam Factory.

I bought a round and we carried on talking about the old days and how it was sweet The Miller was still a decent boozer. And later, when I was back home and in bed, I thought about how I was a lucky bloke and Bermondsey was a top place to live. Better than Dalston any day. You won't get shot in Bermondsey for walking in a boozer and saying something wrong about someone you hardly knew. So I turned over and thought about Magda but the more I tried to think about Magda the more I thought about Claire, and as soon as I thought about Claire the scent of her perfume came back to me again, and I got confused. And the more confused I got the more I knew that unless I focused I would not be able to have a tug, and then I cursed myself and my 29 years. It was a good age to be, but fearsome.

DAD WON BREXIT BUT KNEW HE WAS BEATEN

We were lucky. Dad bought our place in the 1970s when no one wanted to live round here and all the houses were draughty, damp and cheap. Rats cruised the streets, you had to go to Italy if you wanted a cappuccino, and you could smoke on the tube. The house is an end of terrace and Dad paid something like £40,000 for it. One in the same road went for £760,000 in 2016.

It's a three bed with a converted loft and a garden so we all had space, and Barney had his spot in the corner of the kitchen by the fridge. It's in good nick – we did loads of work on it. Mum and Dad's room is in the front, Sally's got the loft and I had a room at the back. We all contributed and there was no mortgage. We were comfortable and we were lucky and the council took the bins. The neighbours were sound.

I say we got on but we had an argument when we needed to. Like Dad was well up for Brexit and the rest of us thought the whole thing was bollocks. He said stuff like "Them Polish builders are under-cutting us," but Sally said that if we came out of the EU the NHS would collapse and then he'd be sorry if he had a turn. Mum said most of the people who looked after the old people she did in care homes were foreign because Brits were too lazy to do the work, and they were all brilliant too. I said the Polish builders were good for our business because they were all hard workers and did a good job mostly, and that meant we had to up our game. Dad just sat there and after a while he stopped arguing and said nothing because he knew he was wrong. And then, when Brexit won, even though he hadn't changed his mind and still thought we were going to be overrun with Turkish or whatever country the paper had said were coming, he didn't crow. He knew better than to do something like that. And the irony is that a week later we needed a plumber in a hurry and our usual one, Bob from Eland Plumbing & Heating couldn't make it, so they sent a Czech bloke called Imrich, and he was the best plumber we ever worked with. He did the job in half the time we expected and when he left you wouldn't have thought he'd been. There wasn't a drip, a spot or a scratch. "He was good," Dad said. "I'll grant you that. And yeah, okay, blokes like him, they're welcome, but not those scroungers."

"What scroungers?" I said. "I don't see any."

"They're in the paper."

"Is that the same paper that promised us six months of snow last summer?"

"I don't know."

"And the one that said we're going to be hit by an asteroid next Tuesday? Or was it Wednesday?"

Dad shrugged. He'd won Brexit but knew he was beaten. So it's easier to believe convenient lies than an awkward truth, but whatever. I wasn't going to let the biggest load of political twattery ever come between me and my old man. I think him and Sally had stronger words but she's got more lip on her than me, which is just as well considering some of the people she has to deal with at her work. She works in A&E at St Thomas's, and the stories she tells would make you go "no". Blokes who turn up with sore throats, women with paper cuts from loading photocopiers, children who've bit their tongue instead of a biscuit. Someone bought their dog in because they thought it had swallowed a key and what was Sally going to do about it? "Tell you and your dog to piss off…" is what she was going to do about it, apparently. And when some gay bloke turned up with an old style Nokia up his arse and she laughed, the bloke threatened to take her to court until she told him she was gay too and was an old style Nokia all he could manage? Why didn't he try an iPhone 6 Plus? So when Dad told her he was voting Brexit she got right on his back and stayed there until it was obvious he wouldn't change his mind. I don't know why she bothered. He's a stubborn man and she knows it but she was that passionate about it and how it will screw us all up and what's the point in trying to go back to some sort of nostalgic place that didn't exist in the first place, or if it did it was full of scout masters who could fiddle with impunity and teachers who could beat a kid for laughing in assembly, and ward matrons with huge syringes, and smoking on buses and every copper was bent and every politician kept a whore in his back bedroom and if you wanted a telephone you had to join a six month waiting list and you could say "No blacks or Irish" if you had a room to let, and no one knew what pancetta was. Whatever, Dad. Let's crack on.

Mum kept mostly quiet about the whole thing. She's the quietest out of the four of us, but that's not to say she's not lively. If she wants to, she'll tell you stuff you'd never think she'd know. As well as her hairdressing of old ladies she always has a course on the go. If it's not something with the Open University she's up the Thomas Calton Centre where the council do their adult education. She's done making jewellery out of recycled stuff, and she's done London history walks, and the last one was about writing her memories. She told us she had more memories of Bermondsey than anyone else in the street so it was down to her to write them down except she didn't know how. So she said she'd find out.

The class was taken by a writer called Charles. He had written a book about the meaning of roads. I have no idea what the meaning of roads means, but he made Mum happy, except when he said that what writers did was important and could change lives. "You think what you do is important?" she asked him. She didn't care.

"Of course. Creating is important. As a woman, you should know that."

"Oh please. What you do means nothing to most people. Nurses – they do important work. And builders. Doctors. Bus drivers."

"Okay. But if you think of the world as a person…"

"Eh?"

"Hear me out, please. If you think of the world as a person, it's got to have a soul, right?"

"Why would I want to think of the world as a person? It's the world. It's just a big rock."

"Listen."

"Okay."

"So writers, artists, composers, people like that, they're contributing something that no one else can."

"Says you."

"They're making the world a better place."

"Oh yeah. Artists are so persuasive. What they do makes such a difference. They really change minds. Brexit. Trump. Putin. That bloke in Austria. They've really helped to make the world a better place."

"We can make a difference."

"Yeah," said Mum, "and I can boil an egg. That doesn't make me a chicken."

I wasn't there so I can't promise that this was how the conversation went and what Mum said about chickens, but when she got back from the class she gave us word for word, so who am I to say that what she said isn't true? And if some writer can get a gig like that and it keeps people happy and argumentative, what am I to do about it? I'm doing nothing. I'm going down The Miller and meeting Magda and having a few pints.

Except I wasn't meeting Magda and having a few pints. She'd sent me a text. She'd dumped me. So maybe "dumped" isn't the right word but there was nothing I could do about it. You might think I was a tad relaxed about it, but like I said, I'd seen it coming. Where she worked she met loads of rich blokes who valet parked and didn't spend the day with dust in their hair. Her new bloke wouldn't wear knackered boots to work and carry a hammer and live in the back bedroom of his parent's house. I think she thought I wasn't ambitious or thoughtful or going anywhere, but she didn't know me. I had plans. So I ordered a pint, raised the glass to freedom, choice and Magda, and when Stu came in I joined him for a bit and then Mo came in too and we watched the match. Whoever it was lost.

THE WARDROBE AND THE KEY

Sometimes, when I think about school and what I didn't do there and how I used to muck around in lessons, I feel ashamed. Then sometimes I feel angry, because I was an idiot. I wasted my time and wasted the teachers' time and it didn't help my mates who wanted to get on that I was being an idiot. I didn't know it then but I know it now, and the thing I know is that like Mum, I'm curious. I need to know stuff. I want to be able to write properly and speak about things with knowledge. I haven't got time to do courses at the moment but I think that one day I will, so in the meantime I just find out whatever I can about anything that looks interesting by reading books, looking up stuff on the internet or watching telly. Like for example, I saw a good programme about how bats live. I think I'm most interested in animals and what they do, so I recorded it.

Bats spend most of their days at night. They have big ears because they don't need eyes because it's dark. So they invented radar before Winston Churchill got the idea it would be the ideal way to shoot down Nazis in planes. But then farmers started killing insects with sprayed poison, and the insects were the food bats ate so the bats died, and then the insects developed ways of ignoring the famers' poison and got bigger, but the bats were dead so they couldn't help. So a bunch of farmers built boxes for bats to live in, and the bats came back and ate the insects again and the farmers were pleased. But Winston Churchill was dead, which was a shame because he'd come up with some great one-liners.

And then I saw a programme on the telly about Winston Churchill's grandson who was fat and some woman said that making love to this grandson was "like having a wardrobe fall on top of you with the key sticking out". And I thought that was funny until I wondered why you would have a wardrobe that needs a key. And then I went to bed.

THE JAM FACTORY
KITCHEN TRAGEDY

Marcus Bowen's kitchen was an easy job. It was going to take us a week. Bosh. We wouldn't push it, so maybe ten days, but we wouldn't take the piss.

On the first day, Dad and I had the old work tops off and carried them down to the van. They were heavy but we didn't smash them up. They were quality. We were going to sell them on. Marcus said that was okay, all he wanted was to get shot of them. Bonus. We wrapped them in blankets, took them back to the lockup and stored them at the back. Then we fetched the new tops and got them back to the flat, laid them down but didn't treat or fix them. I did that on my own the next day. Dad was away doing a favour for a mate in Deptford. He didn't say what, but it had something to do with a boat. He's got mates all over, even in Essex.

I'd been working on the fixing for a couple of hours when I heard a key in the lock, and the flat door opened and closed. I put my tools down and went to see what was up. Marcus had left work early. He looked pale. He nodded at me but didn't say anything. He dropped his jacket and bag and went to the bedroom. I heard him on the phone. He was talking for about half an hour and then he made another call. That one lasted ten minutes. Then he came through to the kitchen, put the kettle on, made a coffee for him and a tea for me and said "How's it going?"

"Good," I said. "We'll be done by the end of the week."

"Cool." He sipped his coffee and stared at the floor. He wasn't right.

"You okay?"

"Not really."

"What's up?"

He shook his head. "I had some bad news this morning." He ran his fingers through his hair. He cleared his throat. "My Dad died in the night."

"Oh God," I said, "I'm sorry." It's strange how even the simplest words sometimes sound so stupid. No. It's not strange. It's just stupid.

He nodded. "It was a shock."

"I bet."

"I'll have to go up there, sort things out." He looked at his phone. "You'll be all right on your own for a couple of days? We should be back before the end of the week."

"No worries, mate. You can trust us."

He gave me a good look. He was sure. "Cool," he said.

"Where will you be?"

"Stromness. Orkney."

"Where's that?"

"Way up north. Just as about as far as you can go without falling off the edge," he said, but before he could say anything else his phone rang again. "Hi Sis," he said, and he went back to the bedroom.

I carried on with the fixing and when he finished his call I heard him in there for ten minutes, opening drawers and stuff. When he came out again he was carrying a small suitcase and a coat. He said "Okay. I'm going down to Greenwich for the night, then off in the morning." He checked his watch. "I should be back on Friday, okay?"

"Sure, Marcus." I wanted to say something else about being sorry about his Dad, but I didn't know the right words to use, so

I just said "Don't worry about anything here, okay? We should be finished by the time you're back."

"That would be great, Ed. Any problems, you've got my number."

"Sure. But we won't bother you."

"Thanks," he said, and he reached out his hand and we shook. He had a soft hand but it was good and honest. Like I said, he might have been posh but he was sound, and sound's all you need to be.

It was lunch time so I followed him down and we said goodbye again in the car park. He was young and fit but the news had got to him. There was a sag in his shoulders, as if the first breath of age had touched him, and he knew it. Then I went and sat in the van. I had a couple of chicken sandwiches, a bar of fruit and nut, a banana and a flask of tea. I gave Barney a piece of chicken. He was well pleased. He wolfed it down and farted. I opened the window. A woman walked by on her way to her car. She was tall and wore a cream coloured suit and a flowery scarf around her neck. Heels. Big shades. Sparklers in her ears. A bag the size of an old radio. The Jam Factory was a different world. I liked it but it wasn't me. I gave Barney another piece of chicken. When I started the chocolate bar he sniffed at it but I shook my head and said "No, Barney. You can't have any. You know that." He gave me one of his looks but I wasn't persuaded. Everyone knows that white bread will send a dog mad and chocolate can kill them, and I wasn't about to kill Barney. He's precious. I found him one of his biscuits and gave it to him, and he crunched it up well enough but I could tell he was disappointed. But life can be a sod, and I told him. "Life can be a sod, Barney," and he looked at me as if he knew exactly what I meant. Good old Barney.

RAMMED MANZE'S
AND ART

Dad and I had a Friday ritual. We'd knock off work early and go to Manze's on Tower Bridge Road. If Mum and Sally could get off work they joined us too.

Manze's is the oldest pie and mash shop in the world. Okay, so some other shop is going to claim that prize but listen – Manze's pies have a suet pastry bottom and a flaky, almost burnt pastry on the top, and are filled with nothing but the best minced beef. There's fresh peeled mashed spud on the side, and liquor poured over the top. You can get eels too, and the liquor used to be made from the water they cooked the eels in, but these days I'm not sure about that. I know there's parsley in the liquor, and some secret ingredient too.

The place was always rammed and a lot of times you had to queue, so we got there in good time and one of us grabbed a table while the other did the ordering. The tables are marble, you sit on wooden benches and there are old tiles and mirrors on the walls. It's as good a place to go for something to eat as anywhere in town, but more than the food there's something in the atmosphere of the place that will lift your heart and pop it on a neat shelf. For a Brexit like Dad it's some sort of heaven, a place where the old certainties are rock solid, the tea is strong and sweet, the Queen is on her throne, the passports are blue and fivers aren't made of plastic. You know, the important things. For a bloke like me Manze's is like that favourite blanket you had when you were a kid – it has a smell that fills you with comfort, and a perfect feel against your cheek.

So a couple of weeks after we'd finished The Jam Factory job, Dad and I were in there having lunch. It was one of those days you get in the spring when you can almost hear summer in the air – the sun gives off little puffs of heat, and people stop and stand to feel it on their faces. My phone went. We have a rule in the family – no using the phone at the table – so I let it ring and go through to voice. Dad carried on telling this story about this old mate from school he'd met in his boozer, The King's on Newcomen Street. The bloke was called Ray Lewis, and he'd inherited this painting of a sailing ship from his Aunt who had just died. The perspective was all off and the paint was faded, and basically it looked like it had been painted by a kid, but there was a legend in Ray's family that it had been painted by a bloke called Alfred Wallis, who was this Cornish fisherman who took up painting when his wife died and he was old. He'd never had a lesson in his life "and it bloody shows…" said Ray, but there was a signed letter with the painting from another bloke called Jim Ede, and this said that the painting was by Alfred Wallis and Mabel Cooke (Ray's Aunt's mother) had bought it from the artist in 1935. And there was a photograph too, of Jim Ede and Mabel Cooke with the painting. "Trouble is, this Alfred Wallis is about the most forged artist out there, so even with the letter and the photo you can't be sure. I mean, the bloody letter might be a forgery…" So when Ray heard that that telly show the Antiques Roadshow was coming to a house in Sussex, he went down there with the painting, queued up for six hours and showed it to this expert. The expert laughs and says what Ray already knows, that "Wallis is the most forged artist in the country, if not the world…" So Ray pulls out the letter and shows it to the expert, and the expert says "Ah…" and then Ray produces the photograph, and it's like he's been playing poker and just showed the table a Royal Flush. "Well…" says the expert, and he pulls out an eye glass and starts to look very closely at the picture. "Well," he says after ten minutes, "I have to say this looks right. You'll need to get it checked properly, have the paint analysed, and the card, but with this provenance, at auction I'd see it fetching 35, 40, maybe 45…" and he did that annoying waiting thing people on the telly do when they want to create suspense "…thousand pounds".

"Still looks like something my granddaughter would do at playgroup," was Ray's response, but it had just gone to auction and someone had paid fifty eight grand for it. And because Dad once helped Ray when he was down on his luck, he'd given him three grand for nothing.

"Top bloke, Ray," said Dad, and he took out the envelope with the three grand, peeled off five hundred and gave them to me.

I looked at the notes. They were pretty. "Cheers, Dad."

"Don't spend it all at once."

ANOTHER CALL FROM THE JAM FACTORY

The call I hadn't taken in Manze's had been from Marcus Bowen. He'd left a voice message that went "Hi Ed. This is Marcus from The Jam Factory. Hope all's well. I might have another job for you, if you're up for it. Could you give me a call as soon as? Cheers."

I called him back and a couple of hours later I was sitting in his sitting room with the lights coming on over the city, and the new kitchen looking good and cared for. I like that. I like to see the work I've done is appreciated. We were drinking the Czech beer we'd had before. It was strong stuff and had a good taste. He said "Thanks for coming over."

"No problem."

"I'm not sure what you'll think of this idea, but I was very pleased with the kitchen, and I think that if you find someone who does a good job, stick with them..."

"Cheers," I said, and I held up my bottle.

We chinked.

"So what's the idea?" I said.

"You know I told you our dad lived in Orkney."

"Yeah."

"So, it's like this..." and he explained that the dead man had moved up there fifteen years before. He'd been an accountant at one of the big firms, and after years of commuting from Kent to the city, and after the death of his wife, he wanted a change of scenery. "He got that in spades," said Marcus.

"Yeah?"

"Up there… it's got to be seen to be believed. But he loved it. He spent the last ten years painting. Not your sort of painting. Pictures." He pointed to the wall. "That's one of his."

At first glance the picture was a blur of grey, white, blue and black paint, but after I'd stared at it for a moment I could see shapes and stuff. A cliff, a distant island, some clouds, waves and rain. I shivered. "I like that," I said.

Marcus nodded. "So he had this place up there, but neither of us want it, so we're going to put it on the market. But before we do that, we need to clear it out and freshen it up. Give it a lick of paint, fix the roof, that sort of thing…"

"Okay…"

"And we were wondering if you'd be up for the job. It'd be a couple of weeks, tops…"

"A couple of weeks? Up north?"

"We'd make it worth your while."

"Isn't there anyone up there who could do the job?"

"Probably, but you never know. If you're going to leave someone to get on with a job you've got to trust them, and after the job you did on the kitchen, we trust you."

"Thanks," I said, and I took a swig from the bottle.

"I say it'll be a week, but it might be two. But whatever, you won't be out of pocket." He rubbed his fingers together.

I nodded. "I'll have to talk to my old man."

"Sure."

"Exactly what needs doing?"

"Well, there's a load of furniture that'll need moving and sold or dumped, whatever. There's a place up there that'll take what we don't want. We'll be leaving the fridge and freezer, the cooker and the washing machine. Then there's a few things we're keeping that we'll want to bring back – some pieces of furniture, some pictures, a few other bits and pieces. A bowl."

"A bowl?"

"Indeed."

"What sort of bowl?"

"It's a Lucie Rie. You've heard of Lucie Rie?"

Sometimes I think posh people are either taking the piss, talking in riddles or both. The trouble is I don't know one from the other. Best play dumb. "No. Who is she?"

"She was a potter. Maybe the greatest potter who's ever lived."

"My old dear would know all about her. She did a course on pottery."

"Father bought the bowl at her last show and told us that when he died, Claire and I could fight over it."

"So it's worth something?"

He laughed.

"Okay. It's worth a lot?"

"Oh yes. So you'll keep your hands off it."

"I'm not even looking at it."

"I'm bringing it back myself."

"Okay."

He held up his bottle again, and we chinked again, and he said "To my Dad."

"Your Dad."

"Dad and Lucie Rie."

"And Lucie Rie."

We drank our toast and he said "Once the place is clear the rooms will need decorating, but nothing special. Just plenty of white emulsion. Clean the windows. Get it looking bright and clean. And there are a couple of roof tiles that need fixing, but I think the rest of the place is okay."

"How many rooms?"

"There's a kitchen diner, a living room, two bedrooms, an upstairs bathroom. It's small."

"My old man would need the van, so I'll have to rent something."

"Of course."

"And I'd need somewhere to stay."

"There're a couple of hotels in town, or if you want to sleep at the house, you'll get a bonus on top of your bonus. If you know what I mean."

"Okay. Sounds like a plan. And you're coming up?"

"I'll meet you there and stay a couple of days, but I can't leave the office. And Claire might go up for a few days. There's a case of Mother's stuff she wants to go through."

"Okay," I said, and as I took another bite of the bottle, I let the idea sink in. And an hour later, when I was in The Miller and Sally and her girlfriend came off their shifts and joined me for a drink, I shook my head when Sally said "You all right, bruv?"

"Yeah, I'm good," I said.

"Not like you to be so quiet."

"Just thinking," I said.

"And that's not like you either."

"Very funny," I said, and I pulled out one of the twenties Dad had given me in Manze's and said "Drinks on me."

"Sweet."

"As."

"What?"

"Whatever."

"Yeah."

LIKE A HOLIDAY BUT NOT
SUNSET CHILLED
CARNAGE

That night I searched Orkney. The first site I found was for tourists and said the place was special. There was no other place in the British Isles like it. Yeah? So Bermondsey's special and there's no other place like Manze's in the British Isles, but I let the obvious slide and ploughed on. I read that the place was spell binding, invigorating, relaxing and welcoming. A bit like Margate then. Made up of seventy islands – got me there – and it's the perfect place to unwind and switch off. I couldn't remember the last time I'd unwound and switched off, and the more I looked at pictures of the place, of the beautiful cliffs and crashing waves, and the puffins having a go at each other, and cows staring at walls, and the long curves of empty beach with blue skies and blue sea and little fluffy clouds, the more I thought that a trip up there was just what I needed. I hadn't had a holiday since 2015 when I spent a week in Ibiza with Stu and Mo. We stayed in San Antonio and if you know the place, that's all you need to know. It was sunset chilled carnage.

I checked out a site run by the local council. This sold Orkney as a place of prosperous communities, dynamic industries and a place where you could enjoy an unrivalled lifestyle. Unrivalled by what wasn't explained but I wasn't going to argue, because the pictures didn't have to make any claims. More beautiful beaches. Old stones that made Stonehenge look like a toilet. Fishing boats with blokes on. Piles of delicious grub. Women singing. Top looking pubs. Families with a smiling blonde Mum and a ginger Dad in shorts and two kids with big eyes.

In the morning I told Dad about Marcus's offer and he said "When's he want you?"

"Soon as."

"How long?"

"A week. With the travel, two weeks tops."

"You fancy it?"

"Yeah. It'd be a laugh."

"Then go for it."

"I think I will."

He took off his hat, scratched his head, put the hat back on and said "Once we've finished the roof, I reckon we can hold off on the next one." We were sorting a flat roofed shop in Kipling Street. It was knackered and taking longer than it should.

"What's the next job?"

"That extension down the Elephant."

"Oh yeah."

"I could do with a breather. Maybe I'll take Mum down Margate. Buy her some cockles."

"She hates cockles."

"Then take her to Dreamland."

"She'd have some of that."

"Yeah. Pass that hammer."

So I called Marcus and said I was up for the job, and we arranged to meet in The Garrison, a pub on Bermondsey Street.

THE YORKSHIRE GREY TO THE HONEST CABBAGE TO THE GARRISON

Bermondsey's boozers have been on a journey. Back in the day when the manor was known as a khazi and people caught a Trafalgar pigeon for Christmas, every pub between Long Lane and the river was a no-go for anyone who wasn't a local. And when I say "local", I mean if you didn't live in a street closer than a dog's piss stream to the taps, you could forget it.

Before The Garrison was The Garrison it was The Honest Cabbage, and before it was The Honest Cabbage it was The Yorkshire Grey and anyone from Bermondsey – or miles in any direction – knew The Yorkshire Grey was a moody boozer with a rep for stabbings. In those days, it was a pint of Fuller's bitter and another pint of Fuller's bitter, and if you wanted something to eat you'd be kicked down the street to Sheila's stall on the corner of Crucifix Lane. Sheila had done ten years for poking her old man in the eye with a hat pin. Sheila limped and sold whelks.

Things move on. The Garrison turned itself into a top gastro pub, and I wasn't complaining. I was in there. It was about a bottle of Magic Rock Inhaler Juicy Pale Ale with a radicchio, walnut and dolcelatte salad, followed by a glass of Gavi di Gavi from Piemonte with the sea trout fillet, dukkah rub and celeriac and oyster mushroom ragout. And I'd have that twice, except Marcus was buying and I didn't want to be rude and I had to be on my best behaviour. This wasn't easy – The Garrison serve their grub in little stacks with the sauces shot like tears around the edge of the plate – but I concentrated hard and think I got away with it.

We ordered. We talked about the job. It was Monday – on Thursday I'd go round to his and he'd sub me a grand. I'd rent a Transit. There was a place I knew on the Old Kent Road. I'd load it with paint and materials and my stuff. I'd set off early Friday morning, drive up to a place called Scrabster in Scotland and catch the ferry to Stromness. It'd take two days.

"You'll have to spend a night on the road. You don't want to push it. There are plenty of places where you can get your head down."

"I'll crash in the back of the van."

"No you won't. You'll get a proper bed and something to eat. I'm paying. I don't want you running off the road."

"Okay," I said.

"I'll fly up on Friday, meet you there on Saturday, show you what's what and then it's all yours."

"Sounds good to me."

The starters arrived. I went with Moroccan spiced lamb croquettes, rose harissa and yoghurt, and he had grilled octopus, caperberries, tomato salsa and pesto. The harissa was spicy and hot and a bit sweet, and there wasn't enough of it. And the lamb was just about the best lamb I'd ever eaten, and even though I wasn't sure if the yoghurt was thick enough it worked like a dream. I was tucking in when I said "I've never been to Scotland."

Marcus held up a fork and pointed it at me. "There are people up there who reckon Orkney's no more Scottish than London."

"So it's not in Scotland?"

"It is, but maybe not. It depends who you are. In the old days it was Viking and then the Norwegians took over, and it wasn't part of Scotland until years later. Even now your average Orcadian is more likely to tell a Scot to boil his head than pour him a drink. But that's not before he's had an Englishman and his wife." He stabbed some octopus. "How's your croquette?"

"Delicious. How's the octopus?"

"Chewy." He chewed. "How far north have you been?"

"Dunno. When I was a kid we had a holiday in Wales. Does that count?"

"No."

"There were loads of sheep in Wales."

"That earns you a few points."

"I get a tad nervous around farm animals."

"Who doesn't?"

"Farmers?"

Marcus laughed, wiped his plate with a chunk of bread and sat back. The waiter took the plates away, asked us if we wanted more beer – we did – and fetched two bottles. I said "I've walked past this place plenty of times, but never been in."

"What's your local?"

"The Miller. Behind Guy's."

"I know it."

"They do top burgers."

"I'll have to check them out. And who's your club?"

"Bermondsey born and bred. You have to ask?"

"No one likes you…"

"and we don't care."

"Get to the games?"

"Not as much as I used to. You can't call me hard core. Time was when they were all I thought about. Then I got side-tracked."

"By?"

"Women."

"Easily done," he said, and our main courses arrived.

What can I say about our dry aged Hereford beef rumps with homemade fries, béarnaise sauce and watercress? I have no idea what they'd done with the steak, but if the chef had come out and told me that they employed angels to kiss the cow to death before peeling the rump off with little silver prongs and cooking it on a flame made by rubbing a fairy's thighs together I'd have believed him – I'd never eaten anything like it. It didn't just melt in my mouth, it danced a little jig and sang happy birthday as it slipped down my throat. "Wow..." I said

"Not bad, eh?"

"Why can't all steaks be like this?"

"I've no idea."

"And the chips. Jeez."

"They're not chips, Ed, they're fries."

"Whatever. They're genius."

"I know."

"Genius," I said, and as if the evening couldn't get any better, the door opened and Claire walked in, headed towards our table and said "Thought I might find you here. Join you?"

"Sis!" Marcus half stood and they exchanged kisses. She pulled out a chair, said "Hi, Ed," and sat down.

That scent again, that control and sweetness.

"Drink?" said Marcus.

"Please."

"Eats?"

"I'm good."

"Dry and white?"

"Perfect."

Marcus stood up and went to the bar. While he was gone, I finished my steak. I've told you about the steak. While I did that Claire texted someone. When she was done she turned to me, ran her fingers through her hair and said "So you're going to be our man in Stromness?"

"I am."

"It's appreciated. You know what you've got to do?"

"Pretty much."

"Outstanding," she said, rolling the word around her mouth like a cherry stalk, and then whoever she'd texted got back to her and she said "Whatever…" at her phone and tossed it onto the table.

Marcus came back with a glass of wine and two more bottles of beer, we chinked and drank, and he said "We're all set," to Claire. And Claire smiled at me and as the London summer swooned, and the chef came from his kitchen sucking on a glass of iced water, and the smokers drifted in and out of the bar, I felt the touch of familiarity and peace, and ease.

DRIVING NORTH WITH
THE RUDE DUKE

I liked driving.

It worked for me.

In the morning I hired a Transit. It was box fresh. A couple of thousand on the clock. Full spec, full tank, valeted. It smelt of raisins and bubble-gum. I collected a couple of ladders from the lock-up, fifty litres of good matt white emulsion, three cans of white gloss, and a bunch of brushes, sheets and cloths. Some lead strips, nails, screws and a box of hand tools. On the way out of town I stopped and picked up a pack of packing boxes from Henderson Cardboard. I chucked them in the back with the rest of the stuff. I reckoned I could get anything I'd missed in Orkney.

It was Friday. July 7th. Hot. I left early. I was on the M1 by eight. I stopped at Newport Pagnell for breakfast. It wasn't The Garrison. The sausages were dead, the bacon was made from rags, the scrambled eggs were solid and the beans had a skin. I had to eat something but I didn't finish it. I have standards. The tea was rank too, but some days you have to pinch your nose. Half an hour later I was back on the road.

I had a load of driving tunes on my phone. I say driving tunes but I wouldn't say they were classic driving tunes. I don't do Bon Jovi, Rainbow and Meat Loaf. If I listen to stuff like that I get ranty in my head, and I don't want to do that when I'm driving. I don't want to spend a couple of hours with voices banging on about how the vote for Brexit was bollocks and if the Duke of

Edinburgh was a normal bloke everyone would say he was a perv but because he's the Duke of Edinburgh he's a charming old buffer with a wicked sense of humour who's supported her Maj for decades and okay, so he said rude things about people from Nigeria and China and Australia and Scotland and India and Ireland and Canada and Tonga and New Zealand and Ireland and Argentina and Russia and Pakistan and China but that's his way and he works so hard and he probably doesn't mean it, and the people who make crisps are taking the piss, I mean when you buy a regular packet you're lucky to get a handful of the things and they say they're going to do something about cones on motorways but they never do, and when they interview someone about some shooting in the States, why do a dozen other people in police uniforms, hats and suits stand in the background with concerned expressions on their faces? Instead of shoving their desperate faces on television why aren't they out there trying to catch the nutter with the gun? And why do they always tell people to pray? That's like telling a starving kid he'll be fine if he licks a wall.

So to keep myself cool and steady and alert I drove to Café del Mar compilations, Ibizan Chill, stuff like Afterlife and Quantic and Underworld. Steady beats, murmured vocals, wave crashes and sky, and as I headed out from Newport Pagnell this put my head in a good, easy place. The voices whispered that everything was cool and Brexit was a temporary madness, the Duke of Edinburgh was an idiot anyway and okay, Magda had dumped me but who was that friend of hers she bought to The Miller a couple of weeks ago I think her name was Perla and she was Italian or Sardinian but isn't Sardinia Italy to everyone but Sardinians? And I think Italy would be a nice place to visit for a holiday because you don't get the same sort of madness you get in Spain, it's more laid back and pasta rocks and they make some good wine, and Peroni is a beer of choice. And you could get a ferry to Greece if you wanted some action. Greece looks cool too and they do great things with lamb, but didn't the Duke of Edinburgh come from Greece? Whatever.

I don't know when I broke my furthest north record, but when I stopped at the Woodall Services I looked at a map by the bandit arcade and I was further up the road than the top of Wales. I didn't know whether to have a nose bleed or feel giddy, so I went and had a piss.

When I was eighteen I went out with a girl called Amy. It only lasted a couple of weeks, mainly because she had some weird ideas about what were fun things to do. One of these was going to motorway service stations because she could, not because she needed to. So on our first Saturday out together, when I asked her where she wanted to go, she said she fancied heading out to Heston services. I'd been expecting her to suggest something like a stroll along the South Bank to the aquarium, or a drink in Borough Market, or maybe we could have chewed some art at the National Gallery, but Heston services? In February? "Along with Scratchwood, it's the only motorway services inside the M25."

"Is it?"

"Yeah. Except it's not Scratchwood anymore."

"No?"

"It's called London Gateway. But it's nowhere near as decent as Heston."

"Isn't it?"

"No."

"So…" I said. "Let's go," because back then I didn't know that a bit of brain trumped a pair of tits. And she had great tits and I was stupid.

So I came back from the toilets, bought a coffee and a doughnut, sat down and thought about Amy and her odd way of whistling through her teeth when she saw a stainless steel bucket filled with two hour old scrambled egg, and I chewed the dough-nut and watched as people came and went. There were lots of families there, some going away on holiday, some coming back from their holidays, some staring into space and some yelling at each other, and the smell of syrup mixed with copper mixed with burger mixed with newspaper mixed with bleach mixed with syrup filled the place.

When I got back to the van my head was buzzing, and when I stopped at the filling station and topped it with diesel my fingers sang, and when I was back on the road the coffee and doughnut sugar hit me like tax, and the world became bright and strong. Back on the road some Spanish tunes calmed me down, and by the time I'd passed the sign to Harrogate, I was cruising at 75. Careful, Ed, careful.

OVERTAKEN BY NORWEGIANS

It was mid-afternoon when I crossed the border. There was a pull-in and a rock by the side of the road. One side of the rock was painted with the word "Scotland", the other said "England". I stopped and got out of the van. I stretched my legs. The sun was shining and the air smelled of honey and petrol. Flags were flying, dogs were barking and people were taking selfies. I waited my turn and when there was a gap I stood by the rock, took one of myself and sent it to Mum. Then I bought a coffee from a trailer, propped myself against a fence and looked north.

The country was wide and high. It was hilly but not as hilly as I'd expected. There were plenty of stone walls and patches of trees. Sheep. Some cows. More sheep. A few houses and farms, and over the whoosh of the traffic came the sound of screeching birds. I took a sip of coffee and was joined by a bloke with a bacon roll.

"Hey," he said.

"All right?"

"Yeah." He took a bite from the roll. It smelled good. I thought about getting one.

"Great view," I said.

"Isn't it?" he said.

I looked at my watch. "You heading north?"

He nodded. "You?"

"Yeah. Know a good place to stop for the night?"

"Depends what you want."

"A room over a pub."

He narrowed his eyes. "You've got plenty of time, so get past Edinburgh. Then try Perth. Perth or Pitlochry. There're a couple of good pubs in Pitlochry."

"How far's that?"

"A couple of hours. But this time of year you'd want to ring ahead."

I rang ahead. I called a dozen places before a woman who sounded like Magda said "You're in a luck. We had a cancellation."

"Great."

"It's a double. You don't mind?"

"No," I said. "That'd be perfect. I'll see you later."

"Sure."

I acted on my bacon roll thought, went back to the trailer and bought one. I asked the woman to cook it crispy as hell, and when it was ready I squirted a shot of tomato ketchup over it. I went back to the fence to eat. The man who'd advised me to stay in Pitlochry had gone. He'd been replaced by a pair of bikers. They were Norwegian and didn't speak good English. I don't speak any Norwegian, so after a few words that were mainly "Hi..." and "Good..." they pointed to my bacon roll and smiled, and we slipped into a silence. I didn't mind that and I don't think they did either, and when I finished the roll I added to their knowledge by saying "Bye". Maybe they already knew the word, but whatever. It made me feel okay to think that I'd helped to deepen the bonds between our two countries.

An hour later, they overtook me on the Edinburgh by-pass. As they drew level they waved at me and the passenger patted her stomach. I smiled and gave the thumbs up, and then they were gone.

EAT THAT THING LIKE
A BAD FIST

Pitlochry was rammed. I followed a couple of coaches into the town and had a coach behind me, and when I stopped to take the turn towards the place I was staying, three coaches passed me going in the other direction. Campers, caravans and cars filled the gaps between the coaches and motorbikes, and the pavements were crowded with people in shorts. They were mainly sauntering and browsing the shops, but some of them were arguing.

I was booked into an old converted mill. I could hear water rushing. The woman who checked me in wasn't Magda but she was close. Her hair was darker and longer and her eyes were bigger, but her mouth and nose were similar. Her name tag said she was Klara and a trainee. The way she worked made me think she'd gone past being a trainee and was the manager. She was very efficient and when she showed me to my room she explained how the lights worked and how I could listen to my phone in the bathroom by using the dock in the bedroom, and if there was anything else I wanted all I had to do was call down. I said "I reckon I've landed on my feet here," and although I know she didn't know what I was talking about, she smiled and said "Of course, sir."

The bed was bigger than my room at home, the bathroom was bigger than our kitchen, and the television was huge. The shower wasn't your normal shower – it was a small glass cupboard with a head bigger than a tennis racquet. I stood under it for fifteen minutes, and when I was done I wrapped myself in two of the largest towels I'd ever seen. I lay on the bed and as I dried I dozed.

There was a picture on the wall of a ginger cow. I think it was wearing a wig. It had been a long day.

Half an hour later I was downstairs, sitting in the bar with a pint, a bag of crisps and burger on order. The light was fading and there was a nip so someone had lit a fire, and as the smell of wood smoke and cooking filled the air, I felt better than good. Some local lads were telling jokes, girls were laughing and old people were looking comfortable.

I texted Mum again, told her where I was and that I had a bed for the night, and she phoned back. I could hear music in the background. Willie Nelson, I think. "Mendocino County Line" probably. She loves that song. She'd put it on repeat until even Barney's covering his ears. "How's it going?" she said. "You there yet?"

"No," I said, "but I've found a pub."

"That's my boy."

"Everything cool?"

"Your Dad bashed his head on a lintel."

"He okay?"

"Yeah. He's starting to talk sense."

"Very funny."

"It's true."

"Stop it."

"No, really. He told me he's going to take me to Margate."

"No way."

"Yes way."

"When?"

"Dunno."

Barney barked.

"Got to go, love. Someone's at the door."

"Okay, speak later…" but she was gone and my pint was

almost done so I ordered another and while the barman pulled it I texted "Pitlochry. Top boozer." to Marcus. He came back with "Great stuff. See you Saturday." And as the pint did its work and I scrolled I saw Magda's name and thought about popping her something, but stopped myself. I've done those sort of texts. They're not good. They never work. Saved by the burger.

The burger was the boss. A wooden spike through a shiny bun, some fat meat, a batch of thin gherkins, a slab of blue cheese, some bacon and a shot of spicy sauce. I knew it wouldn't matter what I did – cut it, break it, beat it or eat it like a fist – it would do that thing a good burger does when it knows it's got you and will put its guts on your lap unless you behave. And it did. It spilled its guts, and as I mopped my lap and wiped my chin, I loved that thing.

THE OUNCE
BEFORE SLEEP

I don't know. I've never asked anyone about this, but when you've had a couple of pints or a bottle of red, and after you've had a shower and done your teeth, and when you're alone, do you lie there and feel odd in a strange bed and stare at the ceiling and think an alphabet of crazed thoughts? You know, those thoughts that attach to whatever they want and lead from a beach in Norfolk when you were six and you found a car tyre and rolled it down a sand dune. And then the dune becomes solid and your thoughts shift to bricks and how they've stayed pretty much the same size and weight for thousands of years because hands haven't changed their size since the days when people used them to build the Hanging Gardens of Babylon, and they were built because the King of Babylon loved his Queen very much and she missed the mountains of the land where she was born, so he wanted to make her feel at home in the desert. And mountains are like pastry, and the crust of a Cornish pasty is made like that so the tin miners can hold them with their dirty hands, and the dirtier your hands are the healthier your gut is. Or is it because the miners needed to throw something to the spirits that live in the mine, because if the spirits got hungry they forgot to prevent rock falls? And then you turn over and the light's coming through the curtains, and you can hear someone in the street below, and they're singing a song and you wonder what happened to that woman who used to teach singing at school who everyone thought was fit and it turned out she used to be a nun. Which reminds you of the time you built some fitted wardrobes for a bloke who told you that two months ago he was driving up a hill road in France and saw a nun on a bicycle ahead of him, and when she reached the crest of the hill, instead of going down the other side she took off like that boy did in ET and disappeared into a cloud. And that reminds you of the cloud you saw that looked like the Queen. And then you sleep, and in your sleep you meet a nun but it turns out she's not really a nun, she's Claire in the dark, and she's wearing a dressing gown. And even though you've never seen the dressing gown before you know it's slippery, and you can smell her in your sleep, and you wake up for a few minutes, and even though you know she's not in the room you can smell her there, as if she's standing at the foot of the bed. And even though you've seen plenty of naked women it's like you've never seen one before because she is so beautiful, and you try to say something but your mouth is locked.

A PLACE FOR
SOME ALIENS

I got up early and had a top breakfast. There was loads of choice. The bloke at the next table had a haddock with a poached egg wobbling on its belly, and his girlfriend/partner/wife had porridge. She didn't have milk or sugar.

She said "You snore."

He said "Whatever."

I went for scrambled eggs, a pile of bacon, a couple of sausages, grilled tomatoes and mushrooms and a dob of black pudding. Toast, a bucket of tea and some more tea. Sometimes I tell myself that I shouldn't eat so much in the morning, but I don't listen. What's the point? Okay, so maybe I'll grow bigger than a house and have to see a doctor and he'll tell me to cut out butter and I'll nod and say I'll do that but he'll know – and so will I – that I won't and three years later I'll keel over while I'm waiting to pick up some thermo-blocks from Jewson, but whatever.

I was back on the road as the sun rose, and passing the sort of views you see in ads for Scotland – mountains and streams, woods and little white houses surrounded by rocks. A few lakes. Some sheep. And then there were some electricity pylons. I like electricity pylons.

My cousin Flynn is my Mum's sister's boy, and his Dad was an Irishman who came to England after the Second World War. The way Flynn told it is that England had had the bollocks bombed out of it and needed to rebuild everything. Hospitals, docks, factories, gas mains, houses, schools, the lot. So his Dad (my Uncle Liam) left a farm in County Cork, caught a ferry to Liverpool and then a train to London. In London someone told him they needed people in Hull, so he took a train to Hull. When he reached Hull there were people standing on the station platform. They were holding up signs for the companies they represented, and one of these was for the national grid. When Uncle Liam asked the national grid bloke what they were paying he was told that if he had a head for heights he could earn more than a doctor. Two months later he was working on pylons throughout the north east of England, rigging and fixing the high voltage lines that would power the country to a bright and bossy future.

It was true. He earned more than a doctor. But with money and confidence came the notion that he was invincible, and risk was a made up word. I suppose no one reminded him that all words are made up, but would it have made any difference? We will never know, for that Tuesday on a bright April day in 1952 when he climbed seventy five feet and looked out over the beautiful fields of the Lincolnshire Wolds, he didn't clip on as the rules told him he should do every time he took a tool from his belt. He didn't clip on and the wrench slipped from his hand and as it slipped he tried to grab it and lost his balance and reached back without thinking and grabbed a live line.

A flash of light, all the traffic lights in Market Rasen fused, and a retired gentleman who was enjoying a programme of light classical music on his radiogram was disappointed. Birds blew from their nests, cows panicked, and Uncle Liam fell from the pylon. Was he dead before he hit the ground or did he have ten seconds of wonder, ten seconds to look at the crazed world? Could he smell his burning hair? And when he landed and ten shilling notes blew out of his split wallet, did he go to heaven immediately?

For Uncle Liam was a good Catholic, and his faith was strong. Or did he go to hell because he'd cursed the Lord six times and hadn't been to confession for a month. Religion – that's for a later time, because for now we have the road, the highlands and a long summer sun.

At half nine I stopped in a town called Tain, stretched my legs, had a cup of coffee and asked the waitress how I was doing for time. I had to check in for the ferry at 12. "Don't dawdle," she said, "and you'll have plenty of time…" so I didn't. I was back in the van.

For the last eighty miles the country was wilder and wider and barer – there weren't as many trees, the houses were lower and the sky was like something you'd see in a movie about aliens. It did that thing that happens a quarter of the way into the story when the clouds start to bubble and speak, and the first few spots of rain threw themselves at the windscreen. For the last few miles I had to turn inland and drive though a flat and lonely place the aliens would have loved. They could have landed their spaceship there and no one would have known, and they could have sneaked into one of the farmhouses and stolen a healthy bloke to do their experiments on, and later, when they'd released him and returned to their planet, no one would have believed the story he told about probes because he was Eric from that wild place where hardly anything grows.

A NUMBERED LIST OF
BOATS I HAVE KNOWN

I have an issue with big boats. I know they float and I know why they float but when I look at the size of them and the thickness of the steel, and the rivets and the cargo and the floors I think something about them is so impossible it's wrong. Stupid, I know, but everyone's got a bit of stupid in them and I reckon it's best to admit it rather than pretend you know everything.

Boats I've been on: 1. A sort of dingy with paddles on a boating lake with Dad when I was a kid and we were on holiday in Ramsgate. We almost sank it because even though I was a kid I was still heavy, and Dad was big even back then. 2. The replica of the Golden Hinde at Borough when I was at school, but it wasn't going anywhere because it had holes and was parked by a skyscraper. 3. A Thames Clipper from the South Bank to Greenwich and back when I was going out with a girl called Hannah. That was more like a damp bus than a boat. 5. The Cutty Sark, a big sailing boat that's in Greenwich. I went on it also with Hannah, on the same day we went on the Thames Clipper. She didn't enjoy that day at all and never returned my calls. 5. A pedalo in Ibiza, but it didn't work properly because it needed Stu and Mo on one side and me on the other to keep it level, so we didn't get anywhere. The one from Scrabster to Stromness was the sixth boat I'd been on and it was the biggest. On its side there was a huge blue Viking pointing at something, and lifeboats hung from ropes. I was nervous but I'd signed up for the gig and wasn't turning back, so I queued up in a big car park and when a bloke signalled for me to drive on and park on the deck behind a lorry that should- n't have been there because it was too heavy, I did as I was told. And when I read from a sign as big as a vicar that I should leave my vehicle and proceed to the passenger decks, I did that too. Now I had a choice. I could sit at a table in a restaurant, sit in a comfy chair in a lounge, sit in the sort of seat that they have on airplanes and stare out of the window, or I could go outside and stand on the deck. I wasn't hungry so I went outside and found a spot by a railing and watched as they loaded the last cars. Then they closed the door, blokes in big boots and hi-vis undid the ropes that attached us to Scrabster, and we were off.

The sea was a long way down but it was calm, and although it got swelly once we were away from the land, I felt okay. Orkney was closer than I'd expected, a fat line of green and grey, and the mainland was never going to be far away, so I suppose I could have swum for it, but when I saw sailors walking around and could see they weren't worried, I went to the restaurant, grabbed a tray and had my second breakfast of the day.

The ingredients were the same – eggs, bacon, sausage, mush- room, tomato and black pudding – and they gave me a potato scone instead of toast, and I went with coffee instead of tea. I found a table by a window and while I ate, the mum and dad at the next table topped up their kids' sugar levels and had an argu- ment about their journey. It was difficult to work out exactly what occurred, but I think they'd shared the driving from wherever they'd come, and had managed to catch the ferry with only five minutes to spare because she hadn't driven fast enough. "But we did catch it, so I don't know what your problem is," she said, and he said "My problem is that you're a useless driver and I wanted a relaxed start to the holiday."

"I'm relaxed," she said.

"Well done you," he said.

"And having a lovely time."

"You can go and play over there," he said to the kids, and pointed to a play area. They looked at their mother. She nodded in the direction of the play area and gave them a half smile. She knew what was coming. The kids did as they'd been told.

Now it got serious, and the man did that thing angry men do when they want to make a point that sticks, and leant towards the woman so his face was inches from her, and his mouth curled and he said "Don't get funny with me, Carol. Get funny with me and I'll…"

"You'll what, Ian?"

He got closer then sat back. "You know what."

"Big man, aren't you?"

"No one's complained yet."

I finished my food and clattered my knife and fork onto the plate. The woman looked up at me and I looked at her. I nodded. She nodded. The man narrowed his eyes at her and then turned to look at me. For one second he kept the angry bash on his face but then he dropped it. It was warm on that boat so I'd taken my jacket off, and my t-shirt was stretched tight across my chest and my pecs were looking good. I gave him a smile. I gave him a smile and then I took my tray to the place where rubbished trays die, dropped the remains in the hole and went back outside.

We were passing an island with tall, crumbling cliffs, hundreds of screaming birds and a few sheep. Someone came on the ship's speakers to say that in a moment we'd be passing something called The Old Man of Hoy, which is a big stack of rock for climbers. A few people came from the restaurant to have a look and take pictures, then went back inside to finish whatever they were doing.

The sky was blue and the sun was shining. A seagull dived towards a bloke who was eating a sausage roll. He ducked and swore at the bird, and went to stand in a different place. Some children came out and ran around for a few minutes, but stopped when their mother yelled at them because it might be dangerous. And then we started to slow down and houses appeared on the shore and we were told that now was the time to go down to the car deck and occupy our vehicles. I was pleased about that and did as I was told, and ten minutes later I was in Stromness of Orkney.

TWO

ON A PIER WITH A TIMETABLE

I'd arranged to meet Marcus by the ferry terminal. I parked and went to look for him. He was standing by the harbour railings staring down at the water. Some of the water was oily but the rest was okay. We shook hands and he said "Good trip?"

"Dreamy," I said. "You?"

"I've had worse."

"It's over there." I pointed at the van.

"Let's go."

Stromness was thin, steep and busy. We drove down a narrow, winding street jammed with camper vans, crowds of people in anoraks and a few dogs and regular types. I parked in a place were the street widened and walked down a narrow alley towards the sea. Marcus's old man's house was called Shore View and stood on a stone pier that jutted out into the harbour. There was a flight of steps attached to the side of the pier, and large metal rings where you could tie up a boat. The house itself was made of well dressed and pointed stone, and had small wooden windows with green frames. The front door was also green, and low. I looked up at the roof. Some of the slates had slipped, and the chimney pot was cracked. The guttering and downpipes were poor, and it looked like there might be a problem with some of the sills. There was a good sized stone shed attached to the side of the house. I opened its door and peered inside. The usual stuff. A folding three step ladder, some garden tools, a knackered chest of drawers piled with half used pots of paint. Some tired brushes, jam jars full of nails and screws, a jumble of hand tools in an old fashioned metal box. I walked around the rest of the place. There was a small garden with a bare bed of earth and some flower pots with plants that looked dead. A stone dog with a missing ear. Then I was back at the front door.

"In you come," said Marcus.

Inside the house was neat and cosy. You stepped straight into the kitchen. This was small and dated but had all the appliances and cupboards and stuff you'd need. A nice old table and four chairs, and some dried flowers in a jug. An electric oven that probably worked. A Belfast sink with a wooden plate rack. There was a door through to the living room which had shelves of books, pictures on the walls, some comfy chairs, a glass fronted cabinet stuffed with ornaments and pottery, and a real fire place in one wall. The gable end had a window that looked out over the pier and the water. There was another window opposite the fireplace. In one corner was another door. I thought this was a cupboard but it was the stairs to upstairs.

There were two bedrooms upstairs, and a bathroom. Marcus said "Have you decided where you're staying?"

"I'm going for the bonus on top of my bonus option."

"Good man," he said, and he showed me into a room which had another view of the pier and the water. "You can have this one."

"Sweet."

"You might struggle to fit in the bath," he said, "but the shower works."

"I'll manage," I said.

"Sure?"

"Yeah."

"So that's it."

"Sweet."

He looked at his watch. "Too early for a cheeky one?"

"Not in my book," I said, so we went downstairs, he fetched two bottles of beer from the fridge and we sat at the kitchen table to drink.

The beer was called Corncrake, and was good and cold. "To Father," said Marcus, and he raised his bottle to the ceiling. "My old man."

"To your old man."

"May he rest in peace…"

I didn't know what to say so we left it at that, and after a few moments of silence, Marcus said "I put a timetable together. Chuck it if you want, but I thought it might be useful." He stood up, rummaged through some paper on the sideboard, pulled out a sheet, gave it to me and sat down again.

It was a list with the days of the week in a left hand column and things to do on the right hand side. The first day was MON-DAY, and under the heading JOBS were the words "Box up pictures, rugs, lamp shades, books, ornaments etc." The second day was TUESDAY. "Wardrobes, bedroom chests of drawer, bed, table etc. to Kirkwall." The third day was WEDNESDAY. "Remainder to van, prep for paint…" and so it went.

"It should give you an idea of what needs doing, but if you've got a better plan, feel free."

"It looks good to me." I swigged on the beer. I suppose I might need a hand with a couple of things."

"There's a chap Father used to use. Joe. I'll give you his number."

"Perfect."

"We used to call him the Stromness muscle. If you need any-thing, he's your man."

"Anything?"

"I'm not sure he could get you a gram of charlie, but you never know."

"I'm past that, Marcus."

He laughed. "Give yourself a week and you'll change your tune."

"What you saying?"

He laughed. "Nothing."

"Nothing?"

"Keep your head down, Ed. Do the job, get home safe and I'll make it worth your while."

"I'm your man."

"I know."

THE AIR OF BARLEY
SUGAR OR PEAR DROPS

We unloaded the van and put the tools, ladders, paint, brushes, sheets, cloths, boxes and other stuff in the shed. I took my bag to the bedroom. I put it on the floor and my toothbrush in the bathroom. I looked at some of the pictures on the walls. They were in the same style as the one I'd seen in The Jam Factory. Grey and black and white with smudges of blue. When you say it like that you'd think they wouldn't be much, but once you allowed your eyes to settle on the colours they did something and you could see the view Marcus's old man wanted you to see. There was a cliff and there was a lake and there was a rough ocean with a boat in the distance. It was clever.

The Jam Factory felt like it was a bash away. I thought about Mum and Dad and Sally. I wondered what was happening in The Miller and I stood at the window and looked down at the harbour, and as I did a shadow crossed the water. The ferry I'd arrived on was sailing back to the mainland, and the mad blue Viking was pointing the way. If Father Christmas had been a smack addict in fancy dress he'd have been that Viking, and his pointy finger would have had a knot tied on its end to remind him to be fierce. But he didn't have a knot tied on the end of his finger and then he was gone, so I went downstairs and followed Marcus into town.

The thin and winding street was quieter now – the camper vans and anoraks had found somewhere to spend the night, and as we walked I was given a history lesson I didn't listen to. I heard something about whaling, battleships, poetry and art, but the rest got lost to the air, which was sweet. At least I think it was sweet – it was difficult to tell. It tasted of something like honey or maybe barley sugar. Barley sugar or pear drops. I couldn't be sure. Maybe the travelling had started to catch up with me. It had been a long day. All I knew for sure was that I was hungry.

We went to a bar in a hotel, bought a pair of good looking pints, ordered fish and chips and sat at tables with a view of the harbour. Some people were climbing off an old boat that looked like a trawler but wasn't. They were carrying wet suits and oxygen bottles and other bits of stuff, and when they were on the quay they scratched their armpits, slapped each other on the back and laughed. One of them pointed to the hotel and they all nodded.

"Divers," said Marcus.

"What are they doing here?"

"They dive on the battleships I was telling you about."

I didn't want to be rude so I didn't tell him that I hadn't been listening to whatever he'd said about battleships or diving, so I nodded in a way that maybe made him think I knew exactly what he was on about, and tucked into my beer.

"Anything else I need to know? Apart from what's on your list…"

"I don't think so. Maybe I should give you a heads-up on the neighbours, but I reckon you can handle them…"

"Which neighbours?"

"On the other side of the alley."

"What do I need to know?"

"They can be a bit weird."

"Yeah?"

"He's retired. Used to be something in advertising. I'm not sure about her. They moved up a couple of years before Father bought his place. They're a bit proprietorial."

"What's that?"

"They think they own the place."

"Thanks for the heads up, but I won't bother them."

"They might bother you."

"I've been bothered by professionals, Marcus. I can handle myself."

"I don't doubt it."

Our fish and chips arrived. The waitress was small. She had black eyes and a flight of birthmarks on her neck. Her skin was the colour of bacon fat. She had a big smile, and when she put the plates in front of us she said "Enjoy your supper," in an accent that sounded like she was rolling berries around inside her mouth.

"Thanks," I said, and a moment later two of the divers we'd seen climbing off their boat appeared. They were carrying pints. They asked our waitress for a table. She showed them to one on the far side of the room. When she left, one of them said something that made the other laugh, and they made those roaring sounds blokes make when they think they could do a woman a favour. I stabbed my fish.

The fish in fish and chips isn't fried, it's steamed. Most people don't know this but it's simple. The batter is a jacket around the fish and the only thing that's fried. So the fish and the batter are two separate things and all they're doing is spending a few moments together. And whatever you do with the batter, whether you add beer or not, the most important thing to remember is to use the freshest fish you can find. I think the chef who'd made our meal understood this. He'd made fat, crispy chips too, and there was a dish of tartar sauce that hadn't come out of a jar.

"Damn good," I said.

"Isn't it?"

"This fish is the boss."

"Was the boss."

"Still is."

We ate and I said "So these people next door."

"What about them?"

"What are their names?"

"Derek and Jean. Came up from Swindon. They'll have clocked you already. They probably keep a log." He laughed, forked a chip, dipped it in the sauce and said "You know what George Orwell said about advertising?"

"Who?"

"George Orwell. The guy who wrote 1984. Big Brother?"

"Okay…"

"He said advertising was the rattling of a stick inside a swill bucket."

"And that's meant to be funny?"

"No," he said, "just true," and he speared another chip and looked at it. He looked at it for a long time, said "It's a shame you won't be here long enough to find out how interesting this town is…" and put it in his mouth.

"And what does that mean?"

"All sorts of strangeness goes on."

"Like what?"

"Well, there's the locals. They've got their own thing, and there's the people who move up from the south."

"What about them?"

He shrugged. "They've usually got stuff going on…"

"What sort of stuff?"

"Some of them have troubles. They think that coming to a place like this is going to sort them out. They want to escape. What they don't understand is that you can never escape from your problems. You carry them with you. The peace, the landscape, the sea, all those things just amplify them, make them louder. Then there's others who think they're going to find something here, something that's missing from their lives. You know, wisdom, serenity, inspiration, whatever. I think Father was one of those."

"And did he find what he was looking for?"

"I don't know. Maybe. Claire and I used to come up and stay with him, and he was painting his pictures, he'd made a few friends, he went for long walks, but I don't think the place made him any happier than he'd been when he lived in Kent. In fact I think it brought on a kind of melancholy. Something to do with the winters, maybe. They're long. Or maybe he was just missing our mother. He loved her very much. We all did."

"Won't you be sad to see the place go?"

"Not really. I think Claire's going to miss it more than me. But neither of us can justify keeping it. Houses up here need to be lived in. They get damp."

"You could rent it."

"Too much trouble. No. Best get shot of it. Move on." He stabbed his last chip, popped it into his mouth, chewed it and said "Eyes front, Ed."

I picked up my glass in toast and said "Eyes front, Marcus."

"And never look back."

"I'll buy that."

The waitress came back and asked if we'd enjoyed our supper. I told her that they'd been the best fish and chips I'd had for ages. She smiled. She had perfect teeth. She leaned forward to pick up the plates, and as she did I said "They giving you any trouble?" and I nodded towards the two divers.

She laughed. "Them? They don't have the balls. You guys want anything else?"

"I'm good," I said.

"Me too," said Marcus.

SMART ORANGE BEAKS

That evening, Marcus had papers and photographs to find, ornaments and knick-knacks to wrap, calls to make and other stuff to sort. I said I'd take a walk. He said "Turn left out of the alley, follow your nose, go past the camp site and you're on a great walk along the sea shore."

"Sounds good."

"Give me an hour or so, then we'll have another beer."

"Even better."

"There's a map if you need it." He pointed to the sideboard.

"I'm cool."

I don't take walks because I can or because the view might be sweet, I'll take one because a brisk walk can be a good work out, but Marcus was right. Here was a camp site with camper vans, caravans and tents, and then I was on a path that curved beside a grey and rocky shore. I passed some old concrete things that had been for guns in case the Germans came, but the guns had gone and the Germans had come anyway. They were in the camper vans I'd just passed. They were very organised. They had tables and chairs out, and polished barbeques. These barbeques were ideal for cooking sausages, and they were cooking sausages. Some of them also had onions on the go, and mushrooms, and I saw bottles of beer in smart coolers.

I met a few other walkers and a couple of dogs, and when I was on my own I called Mum. She sounded like she was down the pub. She was. Dad had taken her out. They were eating roast chicken. She said it was delicious though the spuds were overcooked.

"Good roast spuds aren't as easy as people think."

"These are boiled."

"Boiled spuds with roast chicken? No way."

"I know. It's a bit odd."

"It's more than odd, Mum, It's wrong," I said, and we talked for another couple of minutes about how some people just don't have a clue.

"But you're all right, Ed? How was the journey?"

"A bit knackering."

"And the job?"

"It's going to be a piece of cake."

"Is your chap there?"

"Yeah."

"And you've got all you need?"

"Yes Mum."

She asked if I wanted to talk to Dad but I said not to bother him when he was eating, and she reckoned that was a wise call. I know what he's like if his food gets cold.

"Sally okay?"

"Busy."

"I'll let you get on, Mum. Give everyone my love."

"Of course, Ed. And you take care."

"Don't I always?"

"You know what I mean," she said, and I heard Dad say "Tell him you've got your tea to eat..." so I said goodbye and walked on until I found a place where I could sit and watch the sun set and the waves roll over the rocks and pebbles.

On the far side of the bay or straight or whatever it was called was another island. I reckoned it was the one I'd come around on the ferry, the one with the tall stack of rock. It had tall, black hills. These hills did not look like the sort of place you'd take a girlfriend.

Below me, some noisy black and white birds with big orange beaks stalked the rocks and pebbles looking for stuff. They were smart birds, the sort of birds you could introduce to your mother. I thought it would be a good idea to buy a book with pictures of birds and find out more. I think it's important to learn things. I get that from Mum. When I was at school I didn't think that at all. I think school is wasted on kids. She told me that.

As I sat and pondered, the ferry appeared again, heading back to Stromness. The decks and windows shone with dozens of lights. I could see people on the decks waving. I don't think they were waving at me but I waved back. The ferry didn't make a lot of noise for such a big thing, just a low rumble. And then it went around the corner and I was on my own again with the noisy birds. They sounded like they'd done a pill. After a while they were joined by a load of different birds. These had brown bodies and red legs. They looked more serious than the black and white birds. I wondered if you could eat them. Even if you could I thought that it would probably be against the law or maybe they were owned by the Duke of Edinburgh. But whatever, I did think that they'd probably need about half an hour at gas mark 5.

When Stu and Mo and I were in Ibiza we saw some sunsets from a couple of clubs in San Antonio, but they were nothing like the sunset I saw that evening. In Ibiza the sky was usually cloudless, the beach was crowded with thousands of stoned people taking selfies and although the sun was huge and bright, it didn't do anything truly spectacular. The sea would shimmer and the buildings would shine and the sky would throb for a bit, and when the last bit of the sun disappeared, everyone would cheer and clap as if it had sung them a song, and then they'd spark another.

In Orkney there were plenty of streaky clouds, so as the sun sank the sky took on loads of different colours – one minute purple, then crimson, then pink stripes joined the crimson. The sea turned orange and black, and when, for a minute the sun was obscured by a fat cloud, it shot massive beams of light into the sky above. And then it came out again and blinded me.

I watched for half an hour before turning around and walking the way I'd come, past the place where the birds had been, but they had gone to their nests, I supposed, but I wasn't sure. Did seabirds sleep in nests or did they have little raft of seaweed to go to? Or maybe boats. I really needed to get a book.

When I got back to the house and was drinking the beer he'd promised me, I told Marcus about the sunset and he said "They can be amazing. I always wondered why Father never painted one, at least I don't think he did. I think he bought grey and black paint in bulk. Maybe he was afraid of yellow."

"Can you be afraid of colours?"

"I don't see why not. I work with a guy who's afraid of buttons."

"No way."

Marcus nodded. "It's got a name."

"Go on then."

"It's called koumpounophobia."

"What the…"

"Koumpounophobia. The fear of buttons. He can't wear them, or touch them. Mind you, he's not as bad as some people. Some people can't even look at a button. Take Steve Jobs…"

"Who?"

"The computer bloke. Apple."

"What about him?"

"He was afraid of buttons. You could argue that without koumpounophobia, we'd never have had smart phones."

"What?"

"Normal phones, buttons. iPhones, touch screen."

"Okay, now you're talking bollocks."

"It's true," he said, but he was saved any more explanation by his own iPhone. It rang, he answered. "Hi Sis. Sure..." he said, and he went to the living room to do his talking.

OLD FASHIONED
TOBACCO

Marcus and I had another beer and talked about the roof, tools and ladders. He asked me if I needed anything because he'd be flying back to London the following afternoon and now was the time. I told him I had a hundred and twenty five left over from the sub. He gave me another five hundred, said "Good man," and I got an early night.

I had a shower. I brushed my teeth. I got into bed. The bed was small but okay, and if I lay on my right side and kept the curtains open I could see the boats in the harbour. Lights shone on the water. I heard someone shouting. A bird squawked. I think it was on the roof. The shouting stopped. The bird did not.

Normally I go from being awake to being asleep without knowing it's happened, but that first night in Stromness I sensed the door between the two. I say "door" because that's how I see it, though I suppose it could be a gate. Whatever – it was horizontal and I felt myself floating over it for a moment and then dropping down through it. One minute I was staring at the lights and the boats and then I felt myself go, as if the bed itself was lowered through the floor and then – I suppose – I was asleep.

I had a dream. In my dream I owned a big gold coin that I kept in a velvet box. I kept the box on top of a wardrobe and would look at it every now and again. But one day the box was empty and the coin was gone. I searched everywhere but couldn't find it.

And then I was standing in a garden with a dog, and the dog ran away from me and started sniffing around a dustbin. I went to see what was so interesting to the dog and saw the gold coin I'd lost. I picked it up and took it back to the house where I lived, and was about to put it back in the box when I bit it. My teeth sank into the gold which wasn't gold at all, but foil. And inside the foil was chocolate.

I went back outside and the dog was still there, scratching at the dustbin. The scratching woke me up, but it wasn't in my dream, it was somewhere in the house. I sat up and checked the time. It was half four. The scratching stopped. I had a drink of water, and as I put the glass down the scratching started again. It was coming from downstairs. I ignored it and lay back down and closed my eyes and waited to slip off, but it carried on. It sounded like the branch or twig rubbing against a window. A window or a door. I gave it ten minutes and when it didn't stop I got up, pulled on my jeans and went downstairs. It was coming from the front room. I stepped into the front room. Now it was coming from outside. I went to the window and cupped my hands around my eyes and pressed against the glass.

Orange light glimmered on the water and made patterns like wrapping paper or old skin. The scratching was to the left of the window, at the corner of the house. I went to the kitchen door, opened it, stepped outside and walked down the side of the house and stopped by the living room window. I stood still and listened. I heard no scratching but I heard footsteps from the other end of the pier. They were heavy and slow. I walked back the way I'd come and said "Hello?" but no one replied. Then the footsteps were behind me, or they might have been an echo, because when I went back to living room window there was no one there. But someone had been because the smell of sweet, old-fashioned tobacco was there, and something else that wasn't quite a smell but wasn't not. I suppose you might have called it a taste in the air, something like that taste you get if you cut you lip on the edge of a tin that used to contain tomatoes. That or the taste of beer pumped through dirty pipes, and mud. "Hello?" I said again, and I listened but all I heard was the sound of the water lapping against the pier, and the cry of a distant bird. And when I went back inside and got back into my bed I didn't hear any more scratching, and when I got myself back to sleep my dreams took me back to the garden I'd been standing in before, but the dog wasn't there and I didn't have a coin.

ORGANISE PREP DO DONE

Marcus was a good bloke. He'd done some shopping before I'd arrived – milk, butter, eggs, olive oil, mushrooms, bacon, bread, cheese, pasta, spuds, carrots, apples, some tins and bottled sauces – the sort of stuff that would see me all right for a few days. I repaid the favour by cooking breakfast. He let me have the kitchen while he sorted through the ornaments in the cabinet in the living room.

Success with a building job is all about prep. Get it right and everything should follow. Example: if you want to paint a wall you clean it, repair major defects and apply a primer. Caulk any cracks then apply a first coat. Allow to dry while drinking tea and doing other jobs. Check for missed defects. Apply the second coat. Allow to dry. Coffee. Clean up. The same approach applies to cooking. Organise, prep, do, done.

I checked and sorted the utensils first. There was a solid frying pan and a decent saucepan for the eggs. I couldn't find any tongs but there was a spatula and some wooden spoons. A measuring jug. A whisk. Big plates. Knives and forks.

I cracked the eggs into the measuring bowl, added a splash of milk, a pinch of salt and coarse ground pepper. I know French people say you shouldn't but I gave the lot a good hard whisk, then put them to one side.

I got the grill going and while it was getting fierce I put mushrooms and split sausages on the wire rack. Cooked them for a few minutes, then added the bacon. Whisked the eggs again, added them to some butter melted in the saucepan, got the toast going and didn't stop stirring those eggs. When they were almost set but still runny, I took them off the stove and let them finish by the heat of the saucepan, buttered the toast, finished the grilling and served.

"Marcus?"

"Yes?"

"On the table."

I poured two mugs of tea and he came through from the living room. He had a quizzical look on his face. He sat down. "This looks good, Ed."

"I hope so."

We tucked in.

"Who taught you to cook?"

"My Mum. And I've got a few books."

He cut into a sausage, sliced a piece, dobbed it in some egg, chewed and said "It's first class."

"Thanks," I said. "But you can't do anything with crap ingredients. These sausages are excellent. And the bacon…"

"There's a good butcher up the road," he said. "You need to check him out."

"I will."

"I think you should."

I loaded some egg onto a corner of toast and said "Last night…"

"What about it?"

"I woke up…"

"I heard you. You got up."

"Yeah. There was this scratching downstairs. Outside."

"Oh yeah. Scratching. Thumping. Knocking. Scraping…"

"What do you mean?'

"It's the quiet, Ed." He stabbed a mushroom. "It's what happens when you come up from London. You imagine things in the silence."

"No," I said. "I didn't imagine anything. I heard something. It was real. And when I went down I heard footsteps on the pier. I smelt tobacco smoke, pipe tobacco."

"Of course you did."

"I did." I stared at my plate and then at Marcus. "And it's not silent here. The water, the boats, the birds – it's noisier than the Bricklayer's Arms."

He popped the mushroom in his mouth, chewed it, gave me a smile and said "Maybe the whaler was walking."

"The whaler?"

"Oh yeah. The whaler or the poet. Or the pisshead who lives over the chippy."

"What are you on about?"

"Ghosts, Ed, ghosts. Or pissheads."

I shook my head now, and laughed. "Ghosts?"

"Of course. They stalk the streets, they haunt the piers, they'll steal your woman and drown your father."

"Yeah, right."

"And when they're done with their drowning, they'll come back for you."

"It was a pisshead."

"The town's full of them. Functioning but drowning."

"Not a bad way to be."

"No," he said, and he had another mushroom.

Half an hour later, after we'd finished our breakfast and he'd gone back to his packing and I'd done the washing up, I made a pot of coffee, poured two cups, and took them through to the living room. He was sitting on a chair, staring at the glass fronted cabinet. His quizzical look had gone. Now he looked grey.

"Marcus?"

He said nothing.

I offered him the cup of coffee. "Hello?"

"What?"

"Coffee?"

"Oh. Thanks."

"You okay?"

"No."

"What's up?"

He looked at me, looked at the glass cabinet, looked back at me, and said "I've looked everywhere, but it's not here."

"What's not here?"

"The bowl. The bowl I was telling you about. The Lucie Rie. It's gone."

LUCIE RIE WAS
FROM VIENNA

The short version – Lucie Rie was born in Vienna. When she was in her early twenties she started making pots in a flat. In 1938 she escaped from the Nazis, settled in London, made buttons and set up a workshop in a house near Paddington railway station. For almost fifty years, she produced a shed load of beautiful bowls, vases, plates, mugs, cups and other stuff. When someone visited her studio she gave them a piece of cake. Her work is reckoned by people who know about these things to be the best.

The bowl Marcus's father had owned and had said Marcus and Claire could fight over was made of porcelain. Marcus said "It's the most beautiful thing you've ever seen. It'll take your breath away." He narrowed his eyes and looked at me. "You haven't...' he started, but he didn't finish. I was shaking my head.

"No," he said. "No. Apologies. That was rude of me." He took a deep breath. "It was here when we came up for the funeral. I saw it. Claire saw it. I remember. We were talking about tossing for it but decided to hold off. Mind you, even if I win the toss I'm going to let her have it. She loves it more than I do."

"Where was it?"

"In the cabinet. In the living room cabinet."

"So what's happened to it?"

"It's been nicked. And nicked by someone who knew what it was."

"Maybe Claire took it already."

He shook his head. "No. She wouldn't have done that. Not

without telling me."

"Then you need to call the police."

He nodded and took a gulp of coffee. "I don't suppose it's a 999 call, is it?"

"Dunno."

Marcus got up and went to a side table. There was an old fashioned phone there, and a plastic box that flipped up when you pushed a letter. He found a number, dialled it and said "Yes, good morning. I want to report a burglary…"

Something was said.

"Yes. Stromness."

Something else was said.

Marcus gave the address.

Something more was said.

"If you could, please. I've got a flight this afternoon, so the sooner the better."

Something was said.

"Yes I have."

Something more was said.

"Of course. Many thanks," Marcus said, and he hung up. "They're sending someone round. Should be here by twelve." He looked at the cabinet where the bowl had been. "I suppose I shouldn't touch anything, but it's a bit late now." He'd already removed most of the other objects and packed them in a box.

"Just leave things as is," I said.

"Good plan. There's packing to do in the back bedroom."

"I'll get some boxes in."

"Thanks."

"And then I'll start on the roof."

"Okay," he said.

YOU DO NOT NEED NETS AND / OR BEAN BAGS TO WORK ON A ROOF

Health and Safety rules state that anyone working on a roof must be extremely careful, for more roofers are killed than any other type of builder. They say you should use a scaffold tower, wear a hard hat and a fall-arrest harness system, install nets and/or bean bags, and never work in wind and/or rain. We were sent a leaflet about it. There were a number of other things they said but I used to say "Dad, put your foot on the bottom rung," and then I climbed the ladder. Marcus's Dad's house was low and there was a good wall to jam the foot of the ladder against, so Dad wasn't needed and nor was anyone else. And my head's too big for a hat. Once I had the second section of the ladder rolled up the tiles and hooked over the ridge, I was good.

I started with the chimney pot. All it needed was a scrub to get the soot off and a trowel of cement in the crack. Done. The half dozen slipped tiles took me about an hour. I used the strips of lead I'd bought up from London to clip them back into place. This wasn't a permanent fix – anyone could see that the entire roof needed renewing – but the work I did would keep the house tight for a couple more years.

I was on the last tile when I heard a key rattling in a lock, and the front door of the house next door opened. I stood up and looked down. A man stepped into the alley. He was wearing a pale blue shirt, black trousers and those old fashioned slippers with a tongue and coloured rope stuff around the edges. He looked up at me. He did not look happy. "What are you doing?" he said.

"And good morning to you," I said.

"It might be for you, but my wife and I are having to put up with your constant banging."

"You call six nails constant banging?"

"It was more than six nails. You've been clattering around all morning."

"Have I?"

"Yes." He scratched his face. His knuckles were like fat nuts. "And I think you'll find…" but now he was interrupted by the sound of another door opening, and Marcus stepped into the alley.

"Hello Derek," said Marcus.

"Ah, Marcus. Good afternoon. I was just telling your man that…"

"Yes, I heard." Marcus looked up at me. Everything okay up there, Ed?"

"Yeah," I said. "I'm blissed. Never better." I finished hammering the final nail and then said "All done."

"Good job." Marcus turned back to his neighbour. "You were saying, Derek?"

Derek had gone a tad purple. For a moment I thought he was going to have a heart attack. "All I wanted to say was that I'm trying to write, and that racket was extremely disturbing."

"Of course. I'm sorry. I'm sure Ed will bear that in mind."

"Thank you."

"And how's the book going?" There was something in Marcus's voice that prevented Derek from answering. He turned, slammed his front door shut and a key turned in the lock.

Marcus looked up at me and smiled. "The only man in Stromness who locks his front door. Tea?"

"Cheers."

PLOD CALLS SOMETIME AFTER MIDDAY

Plod arrived a little after midday. I was on my knees in the kitchen. The wall behind the sink was damp. I was wondering whether to do more than slap on some emulsion. Maybe I would strip back to the stone and start again. Plod knocked. I got up and answered the door. Plod said "Mr Bowen?"

"No."

"Is he in?"

Before I had a chance to answer, Marcus appeared. "Hi," he said. "Marcus Bowen. In you come."

"Thanks."

Plod was Constable Neil Murray. He was carrying a black folder and looked a bit tired. Marcus took him into the living room and I heard him talking about the bowl and how it was a Lucie Rie and worth around twenty grand. At least. Kerching.

After five minutes they came back into the kitchen and plod looked at the front door. He took hold of the knob and rattled it. "This is the only external door?"

"Yes."

He looked at the lock. It was nonsense. "Always locked?"

"Not when Father was alive, but if there's no one here, yes."

"And the windows?"

"What about them?

"Lockable?"

"No. But you'd need to be a kid to get in through one of them."

"So there was no obvious sign of a break-in?"

"None."

"Mind you, a kid could work that sort of lock. It'd be a piece of cake." He pointed to the front door. "And you're absolutely sure the bowl was here last month?"

"One hundred percent."

"Okay." Plod made a few notes in his notebook. "And you said you had some pictures of it. They'd be useful."

"Sure. They're upstairs. Hang on…" and Marcus left plod and I together.

I've had a couple of nudges with the law but never been in any real trouble. Nothing serious. Once, Dad and I were questioned about the theft of some antique fireplaces from a lock-up in Whitechapel. Why? Because the suspects looked like us. Turned out the people who'd done the job were Chinese. Another time I was given a caution for smoking a spliff outside a club in Smithfield, and I don't even smoke. So when Orkney plod said "And who are you?" I said "Ed." Maybe I was sounding evasive and should given him the full SP, but I wanted him to work for it.

"And where do you fit into all this, Ed?"

"I'm Mr Bowen's builder."

"Are you now?"

"Yup."

"So you don't know anything about this bowl?"

"Do I look like a tea leaf?"

"I'm sorry?"

"I don't nick stuff from the people I work for."

"Of course you don't, Ed… surname?"

"Beech."

"So who do you nick stuff from?"

"I told you. I'm not a thief."

"And you're not from round here either."

"No, Sherlock, I'm not. Are you?"

Plod kept his cool. "No, I'm from Glasgow. Address?"

I told him.

Saved by the boss. He appeared with a handful of photographs, dumped them on the table and said "There're a few here…" and started to sift through them. "Here's a good one…" and he handed it to plod.

"Can I keep this?"

"Of course."

"Thanks." Plod pointed to a chair. "May I?"

"Of course."

Plod sat. He opened his folder, slipped the photo inside, pulled out a form and started to fill it in. "Okay. This is your case number."

"Thanks."

"If you need to call us, quote it."

"Of course."

"And I understand you're flying out this afternoon, sir?"

"Quarter past four. But Ed'll be here for a week or two. He's going to be doing some work on the place."

Plod turned and looked at me and said "Okay. It might be useful to have someone here."

"And your next move will be?"

"Well, we don't have a lot to go on. We'll ask the usual suspects, but they're all chancers, if you know what I mean. My initial thought is that whoever took it knew exactly what they were after."

"You reckon?" I said.

Plod ignored me. "I mean, there are some other nice pieces here, but they chose the bowl. I wonder if your father was friends with anyone who knew what it was worth."

Marcus looked at his watch. "I wouldn't know."

Plod tapped the photograph. "We'll post this on our Twitter feed. With your permission…"

"That might help."

"And the local paper, they'll run the story. This is a small community…"

"I know."

"… so not a lot goes unnoticed."

"Unless it's noticed," said Marcus.

Plod stood up and said "Of course." He looked around the kitchen and then looked at me and said "Mr Beech."

"Laters."

"Mr Bowen."

"Constable."

THE BOWL'S IN CYPRUS BEING RENTED OUT TO TOURISTS

I made pasta for lunch. Mushroom and herb penne with a good dob of chilli. As we ate, Marcus said "I just don't get it. It was here last month."

I didn't know what to say so I said "Can I have the pepper?"

"There you go."

"Ta."

"We both saw it."

"So if you're sure…"

"I am…"

"Then it's been nicked. Things don't just disappear into thin air."

"Exactly."

"Was it insured?"

"Probably, but that's not the point. I want the bowl, not the money. I mean, what's twenty grand in the scheme of things?"

"A lot."

He shrugged. "Claire's going to be gutted."

"You going to tell her?"

"I don't know."

I didn't have a bowl worth twenty grand. I'd never owned anything worth twenty grand. I did look at a Mercedes Sprinter day van once, and the bloke wanted twenty two grand for it, though I reckon he'd have taken twenty and a half. Ninety five thousand on the clock, full service history and great spec. Sink, oven, 12v lighting, spots, shower, fold down bed, the lot. It could have doubled as a work van, but at the time I had this idea that I'd use it to take random weekends away. You know, head off to the coast, park up, laze around, watch the sunset, throw some chops on a barbeque, drink beer, meet a girl called Sonia, fall over on a beach, wake up at half past three in the morning and wonder why the sky was so dark. But then I was talking to this bloke in Borough Market who had one, and he said a van like that might look stealth but they get targeted. You'd have it parked up and go down the shops and you come back and it's gone, and the next thing you know it's in Cyprus being rented out to tourists. So I dropped that idea.

I drove Marcus to the airport. We left at half past two. The sun was shining, clouds were high and the roads were weird. I'd seen the cliffs and I'd seen the sea and the streets of Stromness, but this was the first time I'd done Orkney proper, and it was wide. Wide and long and slow – we were half a mile out of town when we got stuck behind a car doing thirty. On a decent straight.

"They either go thirty or they go ninety, said Marcus. "There's no in-between."

I overtook. It was dodgy. The road was narrow and before I knew it there was a bend and a lake.

"Watch yourself."

"Okay."

"No, really, Ed. Watch yourself. These roads will fool you. It's easy to think you're cruising but then you're in the sea, over a wall or up the arse of a tractor."

"Got ya."

"Turn right here."

"Okay."

We'd been driving along a good road past lakes and fields and through villages, but now we were on a road that crossed wilder land. Rusting machinery and rotting boats sat in empty fields next to ruined buildings. A few cows and sheep did whatever cows and sheep do in fields, and there were birds. Lots of birds. More cows. A dog. Then we came to a crossroads, turned left and pulled in to let a coach go past. Then another coach appeared. And a third. Each one was full of people with polished hair and looks of vague disappointment. "Tourists," said Marcus. "They'll be off a cruise ship."

"Yeah?"

"You'll see a lot of them. Orkney's the cruise ship capital of the UK."

"The what?"

"They love cruise ships around here. At least some people do."

"Why?"

He rubbed his fingers together. "Lots of it. This place is a triumph of marketing."

"What do you mean?"

"Look around you, Ed. A triumph. Truly."

We drove on and came to a place where you could look out over the sea. There were small boats and big ships and tankers and oil rigs, and the sunshine was bright and strong. We passed a whisky distillery by a bay and then we were on the edge of Kirkwall. There was a sign that said it was a city and royal.

We drove through the suburbs except the suburbs weren't really the suburbs even though they looked like some parts of Margate and were over before they'd started, and then we were back with the fields and the cows. "That was quick," I said.

"There's more of it behind us," Marcus said. "It's a nice place. If you get a chance, visit the cathedral. It's beautiful."

"I'll do that."

Ten minutes later, I was dropping him off at the airport. "So," he said, "all clear on what you've got to do?"

"Yeah."

"And if that copper comes calling again, let me know, okay? I'm not hopeful, but who knows?"

"Plod's plod, Marcus."

"True. And if you need another pair of hands, Joe's your man, okay? You've got his number."

"Yeah."

"Any other problems, give me a call."

"Sure."

"I'm not sure what her plans are, but like I said, Claire might come up later in the week. I gave her your number."

"Okay."

We shook hands. "Happy?" he said.

"As Larry."

He slapped me on the shoulder, picked up his bag and walked down the slope to the terminal. I got back in the van and drove away.

I AM THE BROTHER AND FATHER OF FIRE

I drove back through Kirkwall. I passed the cathedral but didn't stop. I saw the harbour and some ships but didn't wait. I pulled over when I saw an ambulance in my mirrors. It wasn't flashing its lights or anything, and was going slowly. I found a Tesco. I stopped. I wanted some fresh fruit and veg, and maybe some meat.

I grabbed a trolley and picked up oranges, lemons, cherry tomatoes, spinach and beans. A couple of pieces of smoked haddock, some prawns, a pack of pancetta, some sliced ham and a couple of chicken breasts. A bar of decent chocolate, six bottles of that Corncrake beer and I was good. Half an hour later I was back in Stromness.

It was a cool night.

I'd never lit a fire in a real fireplace before, but I wasn't afraid. I'd seen people do it on the telly. It was easy. I found some newspaper in an old basket, some bits of wood and logs in the shed, and made a pile of this stuff in the grate. I screwed up a piece of paper and lit it on the kitchen stove, carried the flame through and bosh, I was a man. I watched until everything was burning nicely and then I opened a beer, kicked my boots off, sat in a comfy chair and put my feet up.

Apart from the crackling of the fire, the world was calm and quiet. The beer was ideal. The view from the window was perfect. I could see the harbour water and hills in the distance. A boat went by. Another boat went the other way. I decided that as long as they kept their distance and didn't bother me I could learn to like boats, especially if they were made of wood and painted a bright colour. The burning wood smelt sweet. A feeling of calm came down. It covered me. I tried to remember when I'd felt so peaceful. I supposed it was a few weeks before when I'd spent the night with Magda and we were dozing in the morning. I remember stroking her hair and wondering if we might have sex before I left for work. That was my last morning with Magda. I wondered if she'd known then that she was dumping me. Whatever. It was gone. I shut my eyes. I felt myself slip. It was a lovely feeling.

I dozed for half an hour. When I woke up the fire was almost out. I blew on the red bits to get them going, chucked on another log and went to make my tea. I lit the oven and did some spuds. Got them simmering. Oiled a baking tray, laid a piece of haddock on the oil, tossed in a handful of prawns, a few tomatoes and some pancetta, gave it a bit more oil and the juice of a fat lemon, did some seasoning and it was in for ten minutes. Twelve, tops. I didn't know how the oven was going to do. It was electric and looked like it might struggle. Then I was back in front of the fire with another beer.

I read somewhere that when a tree grows it absorbs sunlight, and when something like a tree burns, the flames are absorbed sunlight escaping. That makes sense to me. All that heat and danger, and colour. I could have eaten in the kitchen, but I found one of those trays with a cushion attached to its bottom, so when the oven had done its thing I put the plate on that and sat in front of the fire to eat like an old person. And I understood why old people have those trays. They're convenient. I listened to the crackle and the heat warmed my feet.

The tray bake was good – maybe I should have added some more lemon – but if you don't make mistakes when you cook then you'll never get better. And if you don't think you've ever made a mistake then you're an arrogant wank and need to leave the kitchen to someone else. The potatoes were perfect. I had an orange and a piece of dark chocolate for afters and once I'd washed up I checked Marcus's timetable.

MONDAY. "Box up pictures, rugs, lamp shades, books, ornaments etc." I went upstairs. I stood in the back bedroom. I stood in the bedroom I was using. I looked in the bathroom. I reckoned the stuff up there would fit in two boxes, and it would take me a couple of hours, tops. Downstairs would take me longer, but I reckoned I could have the lot done by mid-afternoon. Earlier if I started that evening. So I went to the shed to get some boxes, wrap and dust sheets.

The smell of wood smoke from my fire scented the air, water lapped, a few birds cried, the sound of ropes clacking against masts came from the harbour. I fetched the boxes, stacked them outside the shed and then went to the top of the pier's steps. They were slimy and hung with seaweed. I went down them. When I reached the bottom step I stared into the water. It was clear. I could see little fish and some shiny jelly type things stuck to the wall. Down there I couldn't smell the wood smoke so much. The smell down there was rank.

I stayed at the bottom of the steps for half an hour. Looking into the water was like watching one of those films on the telly with David Attenborough. Have I told you that I think David Attenborough is the bloke I most want to do some work for? Say he needed some shelves putting up for his collection of things from somewhere, or his garden wall had fallen down and needed rebuilding, I'd be there in a shot. I wouldn't bother him with questions if he came out with a mug of tea and a digestive, but I would have to ask him how he always looks so cool in a crap shirt.

When the sun began to set and the harbour lights started to come on, I climbed back up the stairs and walked around the pier. A fisherman in an open boat with a small engine went past. He had a fishing rod sticking up at the back of the boat, and was wearing a big yellow coat. He saw me and waved. I waved back.

When I walked around the end of the house that was closest to the water I reached a place where I could see into next door's living room. The room was lit by the glow of a television. Derek was sitting in an armchair watching whatever was on. He didn't look happy. A newspaper was folded over his knees. His wife was sat in another armchair. She was also watching whatever was on. They were completely still. There was a low table between them. There were a couple of books on the table, and a magazine. A picture on the wall of some flowers in a vase, and some shelves with more books, a clock and some ornaments. A pair of jugs, a china bird, a bowl.

For a moment I thought they were dead but then she opened her mouth and said something. He nodded but didn't say anything, and then they were still again. The scene reminded me of a picture I'd seen in the art gallery I visited in Amsterdam. It was by a dead person I'd never heard of. There was something perfect about the scene, and something odd. Even though I was outside I could feel a tension in that room, and I thought that maybe they both needed a drink or a biscuit.

A DEAD MAN'S STUFF

I started in the small bedroom. There was a bed, an empty chest of drawers, a table by the window and a chair. A smaller table by the bed with a lamp on it. Two pictures, a rug, a glass tray on the table and a little straw basket full of cotton reels. A lamp shade over the bulb that hung from the middle of the ceiling.

I started to fill the first box. I was careful. I used bubble wrap. It took me twenty minutes. Then I made an island of the furniture in the middle of the room and covered it with a couple of sheets. I had a good look and feel of the walls and ceiling. They were sound. All they needed was a rub down and a couple of coats.

Apart from a seahorse made from bits of pottery and broken glass, there was nothing in the bathroom that needed packing. The walls were tiled. All they'd need was a wipe down with bleach. The ceiling was good.

The bedroom I was using was bigger. There was a wardrobe, a double bed, a chest of drawers and a solid table. Two chairs. A couple of rugs. Four pictures on the wall, a set of shelves and a few random knick-knacks. A pile of books. One of these was called LOVE IN A DISH by someone called M.F.K. Fisher. It was a load of writing about food and wine. The inside said she was one of the greatest food writers ever. I thought I'd give it a go, so I put it on the bed.

I finished packing all the upstairs stuff by half nine, and carried the boxes downstairs. Back upstairs, I moved the heavy pieces of furniture away from the wall. As I moved the chest of drawers, a photograph slipped onto the floor. I think it had been caught in a crack at the back of the chest. I picked it up and smoothed it flat. It was of three people on a beach. A woman in a deckchair and two kids at her feet building a sand castle. The shadow of the person who'd taken the photograph could be seen. Whoever that was was wearing the sort of hat you see in old films. I turned it over. Someone had written "Eve, Marcus and Claire, Charmouth, June 1989" on the back. On the wall at home there was a photograph of Mum, Sally and me on the beach at Ramsgate that could have been the twin of this one. Mum in a deck chair, Sally holding a bucket and spade while I dug a hole. I looked more closely at the one I'd found. So Eve was Marcus's mother. She had been a very beautiful woman. She was wearing a black one piece swimsuit, a big floppy hat and one of those looks that said "Don't take my picture, oh all right then." Marcus and Claire looked irritated to have been interrupted. I picked up the book about food and took it and the photograph downstairs.

I fetched another beer from the fridge and put the photograph on the kitchen table. I went through to the living room. The fire had almost gone out again. Being good at fire is something a man has to be. I had a lot to learn. I got it going again. I sat down with my beer, put the book on the arm of the armchair and looked around the room. The ornaments in the cabinet, the books, the pictures and the other stuff would fit in three boxes. The stuff in the kitchen would need another three, so there'd be a total of eight boxes. Add the bits of pieces in the shed and anything else I found and there'd be no more than ten.

Ten small boxes of stuff. So Marcus and Claire had taken some stuff already, but the thought that one life could be reduced to ten small boxes made me sad. I know stuff doesn't make a life and memories are more important than things, but I still thought it was a poor world where a man could be reduced like a sauce. I know it comes to all of us, and if we don't know it's coming then we're fools, but being a fool is comfortable and easy. Being a fool is like being a bed. Or going to bed. Or being a bed that goes to bed. That Corncrake was good beer. I had a shower and went to bed.

I sat up for half an hour and read the book about food I'd found. It had about a dozen stories in it, but they weren't stories in the way you might think, because they were more about things that had happened to M.F.K. Fisher, who was the writer and actually called Mary Fisher. One of the stories was about this restaurant she went to in France where she was the only customer and the waitress was bossy but brilliant. Another was about potatoes and how they're not just food, but the best one was called HOW NOT TO COOK AN EGG and started with the line "Probably one of the most private things in the world is an egg until it is broken." I thought that was very clever, but what was best about this one was that it had a recipe for the perfect omelette. It was so good that when I'd finished reading I wanted to go downstairs and make one and sauce it with chicken livers, but I didn't have any chicken livers, it was getting too late and I did feel tired, so I put the book on the floor, turned out the light and stared at the ceiling for ten minutes.

HAVE A LOOK AT MY
HORROR HAND

I like Monday mornings. I like the thought of a fresh week. I know that might sound weird but when you like your work and you work for yourself and you have a van and your Dad is okay, it's ideal.

So I didn't have Dad with me in Stromness but that didn't matter. I had a van and the weather was great. When I woke up the sky was blue and clear and the sun was shining. The bird was on the roof. I recognised its squawk. It wasn't getting away from me and I wasn't getting away from it. Maybe I'd give it a name. I wondered how Barney was. He was probably in the garden wondering where next door's cat was. Next door's cat is called Floyd and doesn't do a lot. I got out of bed. It was early. Six. I didn't have a headache. I went to the bathroom. I had a shower. I went downstairs. It was going to be a top day.

I made a pot of tea and some breakfast. I had a bacon sandwich with added fried egg and red sauce. It was delicious. I went outside to eat. I sat at the top of the steps to the water. As I ate the ferry went by. No one waved at me. I suppose they were tired. I got some bacon stuck between my teeth but that's the price you pay. That bacon was excellent.

At seven I carried on where I'd left off. I got some more boxes from the shed and cracked on with the kitchen. I made a small pile of stuff I'd need – a couple of saucepans, a frying pan, a couple of plates, knives and forks and cooking utensils, and packed the rest.

It's amazing what you can find at the back of cupboards. I found a packet of peanuts with a use-by date of August 2003, and a jar of jam which looked like an experiment you'd do in science at school. The bottom half inch of the jar was still covered in what I supposed was jam, and out of this had grown a streaky grey mould that filled the rest of the jar. When I took the lid off a little puff of dust blew out and settled on my hand. Now my hand looked like something from a movie called RETURN OF THE HORROR HAND starring me and a woman called Gloriana Ventrinox. I washed my hands and made a cup of coffee.

I could have called Marcus and asked but there were some decisions that could be made without him and one of these was this – start chucking obviously useless stuff. So gross jars of jam, a saucepan without a handle, a chipped bowl, half a dozen copies of a magazine called COUNTRY LIFE, a bundle of damp newspapers and a rusted spatula all went. There were others things too like a broken plastic prong, and by ten o'clock I had three black bin bags of rubbish on the floor and four boxes of good stuff on the table.

It was time to make some space. I took the bin bags to the van. As I was doing this, the woman from next door came from her front door. She had one of those shopping baskets on wheels. It was a warm, dry day but she was wearing a raincoat. She jumped when she saw me. Maybe I should have worn more than a pair of shorts and a singlet. I said "Morning," in a polite way and she said "Good morning…" but before she had a chance to say anything else Derek shouted from inside the house "Jean! Don't forget my prescription!"

"No dear."

"And mint imperials! Two packets!"

"Yes dear," she said, and she closed the door and looked at me and although she was trying to give nothing away, something was poor. She was short and prim with white hair and a tired look in her eyes. She wasn't wearing earrings or lipstick. I didn't scratch myself anywhere and said "I'm Ed. I'm working for Mr Bowen."

She looked over her shoulder. There was nothing there. "But Mr Bowen's passed away."

"Marcus Bowen. His son?"

"Oh, of course. She started to walk down the alley. I followed her with one of the plastic bags. "Silly me."

We reached the street and she turned right. She had to step around my van. Its back door was open. I chucked the bag inside and before she could escape I said "Could you tell me where I should go to dump rubbish?"

She thought about this and said "I think there's a place near the school. Over there." She pointed across the water to the other side of the harbour.

"Thank you, er…" I waited for her to tell me her name.

"Of course."

"And you're?"

"I'm sorry?"

"What's your name?"

"I'm Jean," she said.

"Thank you, Jean."

"Yes, of course," she said, and she was gone, pulling her trolley up the street, and then she was out of sight, like a nun on a bicycle.

YELLOW JACKETS
WITH STICKS

There was more rubbish I had to take to the dump. It was in the shed. Old cans of paint, a broken chair, some rolls of wire and a stack of concrete blocks. A pile of netting and a load of rotten rope. A huge plastic box with a hole in its bottom. Some lengths of chain and half a dozen wooden poles. Two bags of stuff I didn't want to look at. A garden fork without a handle and some smashed flower pots. I carried all this stuff out, chucked it in the back of the van and drove to the dump. It was closed.

I sat in the van and stared at the padlock and the sign that told people when it was open. Tuesday to Sunday. The hours varied. Some shreds of plastic were attached to the wire fence that surrounded the dump which actually wasn't a dump but a civic amenity site. The plastic waved in the breeze. There were no dogs there. For no reason I suddenly felt lonely. I wanted someone to talk to, someone to moan about how the civic amenity site was closed. If I couldn't have someone to talk to then I wanted Barney. I wanted to stroke the top of his head and give him a biscuit. But whatever. I turned around and drove back to the house.

Something had happened to Stromness in the twenty minutes since I'd left for the civic amenity site. The town had turned into something from a film I hadn't seen. I went around the roundabout by the Co-op and once I was past the place by the harbour where the road narrowed and turned picturesque I met a couple of people in yellow anoraks. Then I saw more people in yellow jackets by a statue of a bloke wearing a jacket from Millets, and when I was past the pub on the right there was a crowd of people in yellow jackets, all staring at a gap between two houses and taking photographs. I had to slow down to let them move out of the way, and then suddenly, out of nowhere, a crowd more appeared from one of the alleys on the right. Some of them looked annoyed and most of them were old. Or if they weren't old then they looked old. And at least half of them had poles or whatever people in yellow anoraks call sticks. Then I got stuck behind a camper van. The driver was trying to get through the gap between a parked car and a wall. You could have got a bus through it. The driver inched forward. Someone came out of a shop and tried to give advice. The driver wasn't happy. He didn't want any advice. I wound down my window and leaned out. I heard the driver shout "I can see that!" and the camper juddered forward. The camper stopped. Someone I couldn't see yelled "Oi!" and another clot of yellow anorak people appeared. They were behind me and then they were trying to squeeze between my van and the building either side of me, and I saw that they had stuff written on the back of their jackets. It said "DISCOVER THE EXPLORER IN YOU" the name of a holiday company and a cruise ship, and a list of places. Some of these places were in Norway and there was Orkney and Shetland and somewhere in Iceland, but before I could see the other places on the list the people were gone and the camper was moving again and me too. Half way down the street I saw Jean and her shopping trolley but by then I was too confused to stop and offer her a lift she probably wouldn't have wanted anyway, and anyway she was only a hundred yards from her home. So I drove on, parked, got out of the van and went down the alley to Marcus's house. I opened the front door. I stepped inside. I closed the door. I stood in the kitchen. I thought I might sit down for a few minutes.

THE DIRECTING THING
MEN DO

One day I would like to talk to someone who knows how brains work and ask them why random memories bubble up for no reason. For example – sometimes when I'm working, something I do makes me think of something that's so out there I have to stop myself in case I stab the back of my hand with a screwdriver. The thing I'm doing might be removing a cupboard from a wall and I'm reminded of the rabbit we used to keep in the garden when I was a kid. The rabbit was called Bubbles. We didn't have Barney then so Bubbles had the garden to himself, and used to hop around and eat carrots. But one day he wasn't there. It was like he'd flown away or been stolen by some bastard who hopped the bottom wall and took him back to theirs and made a stew out of his meat and a hat out of his skin. Or maybe I'm having a breather on a kitchen chair in Stromness and I think of the corridors at school and then I can actually smell them even though they're hundreds of miles away. Or I see lots of people wearing yellow jackets and I think about a school trip to the London Aquarium where we saw a man being arrested for banging on the side of one of the tanks and yelling "Come out Joyce! I know you're in there." Or I start to feel lonely when I see a closed recycling and rubbish dump.

I made myself a cup of coffee, carried it outside and stood at the end of the pier. I heard a commotion in the street. I looked down the alley. A 4x4 was trying to squeeze between a post office van and a man on a bicycle, and a man in a yellow anorak wasn't helping. He was joined by another man in a yellow anorak and between them they started doing that directing thing some men do. "Left lock, that's right, more, more, stop…" I drank my coffee. It was strong. I drank some more coffee. My phone rang. Unknown number. I don't usually pick up unknown numbers, but I was feeling reckless. I think the yellow jackets had affected my mind.

"Hello?"

"Ed?"

"Yeah. Who's this?"

"Claire. Claire Bowen?" She made her name sound like a question. I heard a police siren wailing down a street, and the sound of telephones ringing. "Marcus's sister."

"Oh, hi. I'm sorry. I didn't recognise your voice. How are you?"

"Fine. And how's Stromness?"

"A bit mad today. It's full of old people in yellow anoraks."

"I'm sorry?"

"I think a cruise ship's in town."

"Oh yes. Of course." I heard another police siren. I missed the sound. "I'm just calling to say I'll be coming up on Wednesday. There's a suitcase I want to sort through."

"Yeah. Marcus said something about that."

"It's under the bed in the front bedroom."

"Have you spoken to him?"

"No. Why?"

"Just wondered…" I said, "… if he had any message for me."

"I don't think so."

"Okay…"

"I'll be staying at The Ferry Inn, but could you pick me up from the airport?"

"Sure."

"Twenty past one, I think."

"No problem."

"Thanks. I'll call if there's a delay, but otherwise see you then."

"I'll be there," I said, and she hung up first.

I hadn't recognised her voice. What was the matter with me? It was posh but not too posh. She had a faint lisp. Her voice sounded like need. She wore perfume that smelt of water and cake but not really cake, and I know she had an important job. She hadn't told me what she did but I could tell. I might be an idiot but I'm not stupid.

I finished my coffee and went back to work. I shifted the packed boxes from the bedrooms and kitchen into the shed. I stacked them on the floor. Then I started packing the stuff in the living room. It took me a couple of hours. I stopped for lunch at one and had a brie, ham and tomato sandwich, an orange and a piece of plain chocolate, and then carried on packing until I'd filled five boxes. Some of the stuff in the glass cabinet was delicate so I was careful. I didn't find the very expensive bowl but I kept an eye out. I thought it might have been put somewhere safe and forgotten about like sometimes happens, but that hadn't happened. By the early afternoon, the shed was stacked with all the boxes of all the stuff Marcus had asked me to pack, and the cans of paint, the brushes and the rest were in the kitchen. I was pleased, mostly. I was annoyed that I hadn't recognised Claire's voice, but I had to give myself a break. Everyone makes mistakes. So I told myself to forgive myself and went to the pub.

MAGDA GETS READY TO TEXT HER FABULOUS TITS

There were a few pubs to choose from. I went for The Ferry Inn. It had outside tables with views of the harbour car park. I went inside. Locals were drinking at the bar. I knew they were locals because I couldn't understand anything they said. There were Germans at tables looking at pictures of battleships. Beyond the bar there was a place where you could eat. Some English couples were eating there. I knew they were English because they weren't talking to each other. I ordered a pint of a beer called Scapa, took the top off and checked the menu. They did a seafood platter. Half a grilled lobster, a mackerel fillet, some hot smoked salmon, fresh squid and a crab claw with a dob of lemon mayo and a spray of dressed salad leaves. I ordered it. A woman said I could sit in the dinning area. I chose a corner table beneath a huge photograph. It was of old ships. I drank some more Scapa. I checked my phone. Dad had left me a voice message and Magda had sent me a text. Dad wanted to know if I had the keyhole saw in the tool box I'd bought up with me. I phoned him and told him I hadn't and it was probably in the garden shed. He and Mum were just about to go out so he told me he'd phone again in the morning. Magda's text read "Hi. I hOp we cn stil b fRnds. evry1 sed dat I shouldn't hav dropped you, & mAbE dey wer rght cos I've jst Bin dumped myself. WTF! Magda xxx" I replied with a quick "Soz to hear that…" but then my food arrived, and I was already feeling guilty enough about breaking the family rule about phones at the table and I definitely wasn't going to make it worse by texting while I was eating. So I put the phone in my pocket, picked up my knife and fork and got busy.

That seafood platter was the best seafood platter I have ever eaten. Okay so I hadn't eaten a lot of seafood platters, in fact I'd probably only eaten half a dozen in my life. I remember one in Margate that was okay but the scampi was soggy, and there was another I had in Ibiza that was odd because it had sardines with their heads, and I don't like being watched when I eat, especially by eyes that cannot see.

I heard someone on the telly say lobster was overrated and they'd rather have a fat langoustine, and when I looked up langoustine it turned out that a langoustine was a lobster anyway, just small. But I don't think that someone had ever eaten a lobster in Stromness because the half of the one I had almost made me dance, and I don't dance. I'm too big to dance. I'm afraid I'll break the floor. The taste of it went off like a grenade in my mouth. And there was some juice that seeped out of it that was sweet and salt and buttery all at the same time, and if you had some of it with a piece of the mackerel, the grenade turned into a bomb.

When the waitress came over and asked if everything was okay I said it was better than okay, but I hadn't started on the squid so maybe she should come back in ten. I didn't think what I'd said was that funny, but she laughed and when she went back to her station she said something to another waitress and pointed at me.

I know it's rude to stare and listen in on other peoples' conversations but sometimes, when you're eating alone it's difficult to ignore a man at the next table who says "And if your sister wants to come on holiday with us again, you can tell her to forget it. Is anything ever right for her?"

And the woman with him said "She's had a difficult year. You know that."

"We've all had a difficult year."

"So you keep saying. But our puppy wasn't stolen."

"Well if she would leave it outside Boots."

"For two minutes. Tied up."

"You wouldn't leave a grand and a half in a suitcase tied up outside Boots, would you?"

"No."

"But that's what she did."

The woman cut a potato. "Sometimes," she said, "I wonder."

"Sometimes you wonder what?"

"Were you always this hateful?"

"Hateful? That's not hateful. It's the truth. "

I speared a piece of squid, gave it some mayo, popped it in my mouth and chewed. My phone pinged with a message. I had a quick look. Magda's reply. It read "Wanna GIV me a call?"

"It might be, but that doesn't mean you have to rub it in. She's grieving."

The squid was superb.

"Grieving? For a dog?"

"Yes. But you'll never understand."

I had another piece of squid, and while I was chewing, scooped out some more lobster.

"What is there to understand?"

"If you don't know there's no point trying to explain."

And so the evening went. The fish. A text. The argument at the next table. More fish. Another text. And when I'd finished eating and the waitress came back for my plate and said "I don't think I need to ask you, do I?"

I said "No. But I'm going to tell you anyway."

"Go on then."

"That was the best."

"Want to see the dessert menu?"

I shook my head. "I don't think so. But I'll have another pint."

"Coming right up."

CAT IN THE DRIZZLE

I walked back to the house. I was slow, full and happy. Drizzle was falling. The street lights made the world look like it was made of magic sheets. Before I left the pub, I'd texted Magda with "Busy right now," and as I walked my phone pinged again. She'd sent me a picture of her tits and a text that said "stil busy?"

What's a man to do? I texted "Yeah." And she came back with "What's d matter? Don't U lIk d view?"

"It's very nice," I texted and then I turned my phone off and walked on, along the slicked road and stones. I went past a shop and an art gallery and a place that sold things that looked like socks, and things that you might hang off your walls or ceiling if you were blazed. And then I went around a corner and thought I saw Marcus's father's house but it wasn't Marcus's father's house, it was just a corner. But that's what lights through drizzle do to you when you've had a few beers and a seafood platter and just seen your ex's tits. And what a seafood platter. Did I tell you about it? I think I did. And the tits? They were beautiful.

There was a place where the road climbed and the road shone too brightly. I had to stop and put my hand against a wall and take a breath. My breath felt orange. I took another and then I walked on. A cat appeared from underneath a gate, stared at me and the drizzle and disappeared. When I reached the house the cat was there again. It meowed at me. I said "Haven't you got a home to go to?"

It looked at me.

I opened the front door and went inside, and before I could stop it the cat was in the kitchen. I went "Shoo!" but it did that thing cats do, rubbing itself and half curling around my leg and quivering its tail. I said "So you're moving in?"

The cat wandered off.

"Where are you going?"

The cat was in the living room, staring at the dead fire.

"Okay," I said. "Message received."

Ten minutes later the fire was lit and the cat was lying in front of it, purring. Half an hour later, when I went outside to fetch some more logs, the cat followed me. When I turned right to go to the shed, the cat carried straight on down the alley, turned into the road and disappeared, and I never saw it again.

THE DUMP IS OPEN AND HAS FLOATS

When I checked my phone in the morning, Magda had sent me half a dozen more texts and two more pictures. The texts did that things texts do when the person is having a drink between each ping, and the last one made no sense at all. It said '"thy for you ttts and back ar uu". I did think about replying but had some breakfast instead. Then I went back to the civic amenity site which was really a dump.

There were a few skips there, and banks and designated areas where you could leave your pre-sorted stuff. A bloke in hi-vis and boots came from a shed. He was there to keep an eye on the comings and goings. When I parked up and opened the van doors he had a look inside and asked me what was in the bags. I told him. He said "Over there…" and let me get on with it.

I like dumps. I've been to a few. I like their atmosphere and their smell, and I like looking at the stuff other people throw away. Everything has a story, and I like stories. At Southwark recycling I once found one of those carry cots for a baby. It was made of woven straw. It still had the price attached. It was full of baby clothes, all wrapped in plastic. It was sitting on top of one of the bottle banks. It had rained that morning but the cot wasn't wet, so I think it had been left by the couple who I saw driving away as I turned up to dump eight bags of rubble. I thought about that cot and why for weeks after.

At the Stromness dump I found a pair of those orange floats

fishermen use. They had holes in them and the name of a boat of the side. I picked them up. The eyes where a rope would thread through were worn out. I thought about chucking them in the back of the van and taking them back to London as a souvenir, but I had too much rubbish in my life already. So I did what I had to do with the black plastic bags and the other stuff I was dumping, and tossed them into a skip. I heard plastic crack and china smash, and then I drove back to the house. I didn't see any gangs of people in matching anoraks. I made a cup of tea and thought about having a biscuit, but I didn't have any so I just thought about biscuits. Custard creams mainly, but the occasional ginger nut which is, as everyone in Bermondsey knows, the king of the dunkers.

So I sat at the kitchen table and drank my tea and called Joe the Stromness muscle. When he picked up I said "Joe?"

"Yeah?"

"Hi," I said. "Marcus Bowen gave me your number."

"Who?

"Marcus Bowen. His Dad used to live on Dundas Street."

"Marcus?"

"Yeah."

"On Dundas Street?"

"You got it."

"And he gave you my number?"

"Yeah."

"And who are you?"

"Ed. Ed Beech. I'm doing some work for him."

"For who?"

"Marcus."

"Are you?"

"Yeah."

"Why?'

"Why's what?"

"Because he asked me."

"Did he?"

"Yes."

Jeez.

"So what you doing for him?"

"Clearing his house. Some decorating."

"Decorating? Like decorations?"

"No, Joe. Painting walls."

"Where?"

"At Marcus's house?"

"Marcus's house? In Dundas Street?"

"That's the one. Shore View."

"And you're Ed."

"You got it. And Marcus said I should call you if I need some help."

"You're in trouble?"

"No. But I've got to move some furniture, and I need another pair of hands."

"Furniture?"

"Yeah."

"Yeah."

"So you can do it?"

"Sure."

"When?"

"Now."

"Now?"

"Sure."

"What about this afternoon?"

"Sure."

"After lunch?"

"Sure."

"Okay. Half two?"

"Sure."

"See you then."

"I'll be there."

WE HAD YOUR LOT AND YOU WERE RUBBISH

As I've said, successful decoration requires careful preparation. Marcus had told me that all they wanted was to freshen the place up, but Dad and I always believed that you should never take shortcuts on any job. For some people "freshen up" means "slap a coat of emulsion over the last coat, stick some gloss on the doors and hope for the best". For Beech Building Services "freshen up" meant "strip back and sand off all the peeling paint, carefully fill any holes and cracks and sand back, check that any old whitewash or distemper has been removed, wash the surface thoroughly and before applying the first coat of fresh paint make sure the surface is dry and clean". So I started.

I'd been working in the small bedroom for about ten minutes when I heard a knock on the door. Derek was standing there. He didn't say hello or ask me how I was. He said "What are these doing here?" and pointed to some cans of paints I'd stacked in the alley.

"Waiting for a bus," I said.

"I'm sorry?"

"They're waiting for a bus. I think they're going shopping."

"Are you trying to be funny?" he said.

"No. I'm just wondering why you're asking me. Isn't it obvious?"

"It's not obvious at all. And the reason I'm asking you is because I'd like to know what would happen if there was a fire."

"Where?"

"Here." He pointed at his front door.

"Your house would burn down?"

"And how would we get out?"

"On your bicycles."

"We don't have bicycles."

"Then you'd be toast," I said.

"This…" he said, raising his voice now and sweeping his arm in the general direction of the alley, "…is a fire exit, and those… " he pointed at the cans of paint "…are a trip hazard. I'll have you remove them immediately."

"You'll have me?"

"Yes."

"Immediately?"

"Yes."

"Can't I leave them there for a few more minutes?"

"Why?"

"In case the bus arrives."

Derek narrowed his eyes. His cheeks started to colour. He made a cat's arse with his mouth. He said "When we left Swindon I thought we'd left people like you behind."

"Swindon?"

"Yes."

I laughed. "We had you. 1-0. League One play-off final, 2010. Paul Robinson in the 39th minute. You were rubbish."

Now I think Derek thought I might have been talking Chinese. He shook his head, turned, pointed at the cans of paint, hissed "Move them!" and went back to the house.

I was going to bring the cans in anyway so I did, and stacked them in the corner of the kitchen, made myself a cup of coffee and went upstairs to carry on the prep.

I listen to the radio when I work. When I'm with Dad it's usually talkRADIO, where personalities talk about things and men like Derek phone up to complain about supermarket car parks. When I'm on my own I listen to Chill or 6 Music, but I couldn't get Chill in Stromness and 6's signal was poor, so I went for Radio 1 until I thought I was going to go mad. So I docked my phone and listened to some tunes from Underworld's new one, finished washing down the small bedroom and started on the one I was using. I'd done by lunch time so went to make myself some bacon and scrambled eggs. Two pieces of toast and maybe some mushrooms. I was hungry.

MILK, SIX SUGARS, TWENTY GRAND

I was eating the last mushroom when there was a knock on the door. I got ready to come up with an answer to whatever Derek wanted to complain about, but the knocker was Joe.

I'm big but Joe was massive. When I opened the door he blocked out the light and I had to peer out and up to see his head. He looked down at me and said "Hello".

"Hi," I said. "Joe?"

"That's me."

"Come in," I said, "if you can."

He bent down and stepped into the kitchen.

"Cup of tea?"

"Thanks." He pulled out a chair and sat down. "You've got some furniture you want to move?"

"I do."

"Know where you want to take it?"

"No. It's too good to take to the dump, but Marcus doesn't want anything for it, so I was hoping you'd know somewhere."

"There's Restart in Kirkwall. It's like a charity that helps people get work. What have you got?"

"A wardrobe, a couple of chests. A table. Armchairs, stuff like that."

"Yeah, they'll have it."

The kettle boiled. I started to make the tea. "How'd you like it?"

"Milk. Six sugars."

"I've got to go to Kirkwall tomorrow, so if you could help me get the stuff in the back of the van, that'd be great. Restart, yeah?"

"Junction Road. You can't miss it."

"I'll find it."

I put the tea in front of him. "Thanks."

I held my mug up to his, said "Cheers" and sat down.

He looked around the kitchen and said "I was sad when old Mr Bowen died. He was a good bloke. Gave me one or two jobs. I'll miss him. Marcus is selling the place?"

"Yeah."

"It'll go like that." He clicked his fingers and sipped his tea. "The old man had a few nice things too."

"He did. And you're not the only one who thought so."

"What you mean?"

I stood up, went to the living room and fetched the photographs of the bowl plod hadn't taken. I put them on the kitchen table and said "See that?"

"It's a bowl."

"Yeah."

"What about it?"

"What you reckon it's worth?"

He shrugged. "A fiver?"

"Twenty grand."

"You're kidding."

"No."

"Twenty grand?"

I nodded. "Minimum. It was one of the old man's treasures. Used to live in the living room, except it's disappeared. Marcus reckons it's been nicked."

"No way."

"We had the police round."

"Nicked?"

"That's what he reckons."

"Interesting…"

"Why interesting?"

"Can I take one of these pictures?"

"Why?"

"I want to show it to my missus."

"Your missus? What does she know about it?"

"My Ellen knows everything."

"Yeah?"

"Oh yes. And if she doesn't, she'll know someone who does."

"Sweet."

Half an hour later, we had the furniture in the van, and I was standing in the street with Joe. I'd palmed him a twenty and he looked at the note and said "You sure?"

"Marcus is paying," I said, " and he's the sort of guy who drops those for fun."

"Cool," said Joe. "You know The Ferry?"

"The pub?"

"That's the one."

"We'll be up there later if you fancy a pint."

"You're on."

BOUGHT BY NOBS, OBVS

After Joe left I felt tired. Maybe it I was suffering from a serious illness that would kill me within six months or maybe I was tired. I've often thought that I'll die of one of those odd things that attack your blood and make you thin, either that or in a road accident involving a horse. Maybe I needed to talk to my mum. I called her. She didn't pick up, so I called Sally but went through to voicemail. I left her a message. I said "Hi Sal. Everything okay? Love you." I called Dad. He didn't pick up either. I didn't leave him a message. I wished Barney had a phone. He would have picked up but had paws so wouldn't have been able to use the buttons and/or touch screen. So then I thought I'd go upstairs and see if the walls were dry. They were. The bed in the room I was using looked very comfortable so I lay down for five minutes. An hour later I woke up. I definitely had a serious illness that would kill me within six months, so I went for a drive. I would go for a drive and then I'd go for a walk. Fresh air is good for people with a terminal illness.

I drove out of town and followed the signs to a thing called Skara Brae. I'd read about it in a magazine on the ferry, and seen pictures. It's an old place. There were loads of coaches in the car park and too many cars to count. I went to the place where you paid and gave a women my money and then I could go to where the stuff I had to see was. These were next to the sea and were mostly big holes in the ground and stone walls, and mounds of earth. There were also hundreds and hundreds of people wandering around, staring and taking selfies. Some of these people were in yellow anoraks and a few others were wearing blue and orange anoraks, and there were some others who were just normal tourists who didn't have to wear a uniform. Some guide people were there too. I stood on a hump and looked down at one of the holes in the ground that had once been a house but would need work if you wanted to live in it now. It had a shelf and a place where someone could have slept, and a fireplace. I got the feeling that the whole place was made up like the Flintstones. It was like some farmer had lost all his sheep in an accident and woken up in the middle of the night a few days later and thought "I'll make an old village in the sand dunes at the bottom of that useless field, tell some nobs from England that I've discovered the ruins of somewhere that was built before anyone even thought about the pyramids and I'll be quids in." And stone me if the nobs didn't buy it and everyone since, and now hundreds of thousands of people have bought it too, and the soup in the attached café isn't bad but that pencil sharpener shaped like a dinosaur egg is rubbish. However not all was lost. They had a load of books there and one of them was about the birds of Orkney. It had some great pictures and all the stuff you needed to know about what the birds did, where they lived, what they ate and where they went when they weren't where you expected them to be. It was called THE ORKNEY BOOK OF BIRDS and cost £9.99. I bought it, and when the woman asked me if I wanted a bag I said "No thanks," and put it in my jacket pocket. Then I left Skara Brae, got back in the van and drove back to Stromness, and within an hour the symptoms of my terminal illness had passed, and I was okay to drink beer.

BUTCH CASSIDY AND
THE SUNDANCE KID
WHATEVER

Apart from imagining that real things are made up, and needing to do a good job when I'm working, and liking to cook to a high standard, and thinking that I'm going to die of an unusual blood disease, and wanting to learn about birds, I suffer from a thing that makes me worry about what would have happened if something hadn't been made or discovered. So, for example, I'll worry about what would have happened if the recipe for beer hadn't been worked out. I know it has been so what's the point, but I want to know who made the first pint. And how long did it take them to work out that if you take water, barley, hops and yeast and mix them together in the right quantities you'll end up with something that tastes great and gets you drunk? And what sort of stuff did they try mixing together before they came up with the right stuff? Earth? Bark? Some leaves?

I calmed myself by sitting in a corner of The Ferry with a pint and my bird book. I worked out that the noisy black and white birds with orange beaks are called Oyster Catchers, and the ones with red legs are Red Shanks. The Oyster Catchers are posh looking and were my favourite so far.

I was on my second pint and looking at the menu and wondering if I might have a bowl of seafood chowder when Joe and his missus turned up. I went over and he said "Hi Ed. This is Ellen."

I said "Hi Ellen."

She said. "All right?"

"Yeah," I said. "What you want?"

"Pint of Scapa," she said.

"Joe?"

"Me too."

I said "Two pints of Scapa..." to the barman and a few minutes later we were sitting at my table and a bunch of divers at the next table were talking about their stuff and Sky was on with the sound down.

Ellen was all no nonsense and wavy hands. She wasn't as big as Joe but she would have punished a moped, and it didn't take her long to get to the point. It took her two minutes. She had half her pint down her neck and then she said "So there's a bowl worth twenty grand?"

"Yeah," I said.

"That's mental."

I was so careful I didn't breathe.

"And it's gone missing."

"Nicked, we reckon."

"Is there a reward?"

Good question. "Good question," I said. "I don't know, but it wouldn't surprise me."

"There should be."

"You're right about that."

"At least a grand."

"A grand?"

"I reckon."

Joe looked at his missus and looked at me, then looked back at me.

"So?" I said.

"So what?" Ellen said. As well as wavy hands she had huge

red hair and fat lips. She made me shudder and twinge at the same time. I've had that feeling with some women. It's an odd one.

"You want me to find out?

"Find out what?"

"If there's a reward?"

"I think you should."

"Why?"

"Well, it's like Butch Cassidy and that, isn't it?"

"Butch Cassidy?"

"Yeah. No one's going to turn him in unless there's money in it, are they?"

"I suppose not."

"So if there's this bowl and it's worth a fortune, someone's going to want it back, aren't they?"

"But it's not about the money."

"Then what the hell is it about?"

Joe was still quiet.

I was going to explain but then I thought I wouldn't, and I'd go outside and call Marcus, which is what I did.

So I went outside and strolled towards the harbour and called Marcus as the ferry appeared, and when he picked up and asked how things were I said "It's odd."

He laughed. "What did I tell you?"

"Joe came round this afternoon."

"He's a good chap, isn't he?"

"Yeah. And now I'm in the pub with him and his missus."

"Sounds friendly."

"Oh yes," I said. "It is…" and I told him I'd told Joe about the bowl and he'd told his missus and now she was asking if there was a reward.

"A reward?"

"Yeah."

"Why's she asking that?"

"I don't know."

"Does she know something?"

"Who knows?"

"Well," said Marcus, "If we get it back in one piece, I suppose there could be."

"She thinks any reward's got to be a grand."

"Does she?"

"Yeah."

"A grand?"

"Yeah."

He thought about it for a minute. Cars and lorries and bikes rolled off the ferry. "Well, if it gets the thing back…"

"I don't know if she's trying it on," I said, "or if she knows anything. It's hard to say."

"Well no one's getting anything until I've got the bowl in my hands, so it's no skin off my nose."

"True."

"Tell her that."

"Okay," so I did, and she smiled and told me that maybe she did know something but maybe she didn't.

"Here's the thing," I explained. I talked slowly. She nodded. "This isn't a game. If you know something, tell me. If you don't, then no one cares. It's that simple."

She stared at me. I waited as this information sunk in. It took a while. Joe nodded. "Okay," she said. "And if I do know something, then what?"

I shrugged. "You tell me?"

"And when do I get the money?"

"Like I said, Marcus gets the bowl, you get the money."

She downed the rest of her pint, put the empty glass on the table, licked her lips and looked at me. She was struggling. "If I tell you something, how do I know I can trust you? I mean, I don't know you from Adam."

I shook my head. I had nothing else to say and now she knew it. She looked at Joe. Joe looked at her. He said "Tell him."

"Yeah," I said. "Tell me."

She looked at her pint. "Buy me another and I will."

"Tell me," I said, "and I will."

ELLEN DOES SOME CLEANING

"I clean for this couple in town. He's from round here, used to be a Captain on a ship. She's German or something."

"Dutch," said Joe. "She's Dutch."

"Whatever, Joe. Elise and Alec. They never give me any grief, pay good money, you know, but he's weird."

"Weird?"

"Yeah. I mean, when I'm working round there she's okay and she'll talk and everything, but he spends all his time in this place he's got, and if I do see him he never says a word. He's, you know, shifty."

"Is he?"

"Yeah. Always looks sideways at me."

"Maybe he's just shy."

"Yeah, right."

"And this place? What is it?"

"Well it's in the garden but it's not a shed, and it's not a garage. It's more like just a room on its own, if you know what I mean. It's got proper windows and everything."

"Okay."

"So last week I was taking some rubbish to the bin, and had to go down past this place. He was in there doing whatever he does, and usually he keeps the door closed but this time it was open, so I could see in. And there were loads of pictures and books and shelves in there, and I saw that bowl."

"Which bowl?"

"The one in the photo you gave Joe."

"You sure?"

"For definite."

"Where?"

"On one of the shelves. Just sitting there. There were loads of others, but old man Bowen's was one of them."

"And what makes you sure it was the one in the photo?"

"It's unusual, isn't it? That green stuff on it. You know, it stands out."

"It certainly does."

"And he was friendly with Mr Bowen," said Joe. "He was down there all the time."

"Was he?"

"Oh yes."

"So what I'm thinking…" said Ellen, "… is that he saw it one day and he knew what it was worth and…"

"You don't need to spell it out," I said.

"No?"

"I don't think so. And Elise and Alec live where?"

"You know where the museum is?"

"Yeah."

"So you go past the museum, and they're at the South End. You can't miss the house. It's got a plastic owl on the roof."

"Okay," I said, and I finished my pint. "Scapa?"

"And a shot of Highland Park," she said.

"Joe?"

"Same."

I got the drinks in. It all sounded too simple, but sometimes simple is the solution. Like when you ask people what colour they want their bathroom and the woman says she wants it Prussian

Blue and the man says he wants it Ocean Grey and they have a fight and you suggest they go for white because it's a small room. But which white? Frosted Hint or Plain Cloud? Just plain trade white emulsion with a hint of white. Please? Thank you.

Scapa was a good pint. "Why've they got a plastic owl on the roof?" I said.

"It's meant to scare the gulls away," said Joe, "but I saw one sat on it once."

"Gulls aren't stupid," said Ellen.

"Yes they are," said Joe. "They're idiots."

"Yeah, but they aren't stupid."

"And this place. This room. Where is it?"

"Behind the house," said Ellen.

"Okay."

"So what's the plan?"

"I don't know yet, but you'll be the first to know."

"We'd better be," said Ellen.

"Oh leave it," said Joe.

"Why? Are we going to trust him? He's English."

"No I'm not," I said.

"What are you?"

"German," I said, and Ellen did that twitchy thing people do with their heads when they're not sure what's happened. Then she went quiet.

BOOTY AND BOWLY

Whisky takes me to a dark place, but that doesn't stop me drinking the stuff. I suppose it's like ducks knowing they should not eat white bread because it will make them explode, but they still do. So when I saw Joe and Ellen having a shot of Highland Park and they told me it had won prizes and the best way to drink it was with a pint, I got another round in, and doubles. And they were right. It had won prizes. The barman said so.

An hour later I was walking back to old man Bowen's soon to be sold house and saying goodnight to Joe and Ellen who lived up Hellihole Road, and then I was past there and doing that thing when you point at street lights for no reason, and the lights wink and you think they hate you. And the dark place is long and hard, and your legs are logs, and the logs are dark, and the world is made of feet. And a cat you think you recognise from a day or two ago is leading you on and up, past the house where you're meant to stop and sleep, and past the bend and the museum, and then a wall by a lawn or is it a beach? And you can hear water running. And then what? What is that other noise? Who is shining those lights? It's a car, and why are people shouting at you? And what is this gate, and why is there an owl on the roof of that house?

The owl on the roof made me stop and fall over. I was in a flowerbed. I got up. I was in a bush. Then I was in another bush. I fell over again. I was in the flowerbed again. I looked up. The plastic owl looked at me. It had plastic eyes. I thought about having a snooze. I closed my eyes. I tasted medicine and apples. Everything swam so I opened my eyes and stood up. I could see.

That was better. I stepped out of the flower bed and onto a garden path. The path was grey and straight and sloped up. It spoke to me. I listened. I did what it told me to do. I walked up it until I reached the front door of a house. I could hear people talking inside but I couldn't hear what they were saying. I looked up. The plastic owl was still there. It wanted me to knock on the door so I did. I looked at my feet. I was only wearing one boot. The door opened. A man was standing there. He looked okay. He said "Yes?" so I said "Have you seen my boot?"

"I'm sorry?" said the man. A woman appeared behind him. She was wearing a dressing gown and a knitted hat with a tall pointy bit on her head. She looked like a big doll on acid. She said "Who is this?"

"A young man who's lost his boot," said the man.

"Oh dear," said the woman. "That won't do."

"My bowl," I said, "and my bowl. I've lost my bowl."

"Your boot and your bowl?" said the man. "My word. I'd say you were in something of a pickle."

"Yes," I said. "I am very."

The woman leant towards the man and said something to him. The man pointed down the garden path and said "Is that your boot?" I turned around. It wasn't easy. I looked and yes, it was my boot.

"My boot!" I cried. "It's waiting for me." I walked towards it and crouched down and picked it up and looked at it. "Hello booty," I said.

The man had followed me. "All's well that ends well," he said.

"What?" I said.

"Now all you need is your bowl. Maybe you left it at home? Where do you live?"

"Down there," I pointed at the sea. Lights were twinkling. "No.

Over there." I pointed at the sky. More lights were twinkling. I turned back and looked at the man. Lights were everywhere. I loved all the lights and their twinkling. "But it's not at home. You've got it. You've got bowly."

"Well," said the man, "we've got lots of bowls, but I don't think we've got yours."

"You…" I said, as I tried to stand on one leg and put my boot on and point and focus and think, "have got lovely bowly…"

"Well," the man said, "why don't you come back tomorrow and we'll talk about it, and maybe have a look for it."

"Okay," I said. "And I'll bring booty," and I fell over.

"Ooops," said the man.

"It's okay," I said, and I sat up. Now it was easier to get booty on my foot, so I did. And then I stood up again and headed down the path. "I'm going home now," I said, and I pointed at the sky. The stars were blinding, and I heard a bird. I thought it was an antelope or fish.

"Good for you," said the man.

"Laters!" I cried, and I raised my arm in triumph. I was going to solve the case of missing bowly. I was like that old woman who lives in a village where everyone kills everyone else but always finds the murderer and eats cakes.

IF JESUS HAD HAD A GUN HE'D BE ALIVE TODAY

I did not feel good in the morning. I had a bruise on my forehead and there was earth in my hair. My mouth left like someone had been in there with a belt sander, and a family of ants had set up home in my brain. They were playing bad jazz with spoons on saucepans. But I'm strong for a reason. A pint of water, a shower, a bucket of tea and a fry-up sorted me. Eggs, bacon, two sausages, a dob of baked beans and two pieces of toast. That and some work with the windows open. Ideal.

The paint went on well and I did loads. I made a cup of coffee at eleven, stepped outside and looked at the harbour. As I was staring at the water and sipping the coffee, Jean came from next door with a basket and started to peg some clothes on her washing line. I said "Morning…" in a polite way. She jumped and dropped her bag of pegs. I went over to help her pick them up, but she said she could manage so I went back to my sipping. She worked in a very methodical way, pegging socks in their pairs, a pair of shirts together, and a pair of trousers next. When she'd finished she went back to the house with her washing basket under her arm, and didn't say "Goodbye" or "See you later" or anything at all. She was a very quiet woman.

An hour later I took the furniture to Kirkwall. As I drove round the last bend before the town I saw a cruise ship. It was tied up to a jetty. I'd never seen such a big boat. It had hundreds of windows and big funnels and stubby masts and white globe things on its roof. Just looking at it made me nervous and ask too many questions. What did it weigh? When it was full of people how much more did it weigh? How much would it have to weigh before it sank?

When I reached the turning that led down to the place where the boat was tied up, I had to slow down because a bendy bus full of passengers was pulling out. I'd been told that after Boris got rid of them, London's bendy buses ended up in Malta but here was one in Kirkwall taking large people to see the sights of Orkney, and there was another behind me. And suddenly there was another, coming back the other way. It was all too confusing. I wanted some sense in my life.

Joe had been right. The Restart place was difficult to miss. It was a big building full of cheap stuff, furniture mainly, but also lots of cushions. Two blokes and a woman came out to help me unload. They were pleased to see me. When I told them that I might bring them some more stuff the smaller of the two blokes said "Bring it on." I said I would and then I drove to Tesco. I bought some food, some bottles of beer and wine, left the van in the car park, walked into town and took a turn around the cathedral.

Marcus had been right. It was beautiful. The builders knew what they were doing. Massive stone columns held up the roof. Most of the windows were made of coloured glass but there was one made from plain glass, and the sun shone through it and threw floods and coins of light onto the columns and the floor. Someone had done some great wood carving on some benches and chairs, and there were old gravestones attached to the walls.

Hundreds of other people had had the same idea as me and were in there, taking photos and talking about how old the place was. There were loads of hungry Americans. Most of them were fat and wearing leggings and/or sweats with stuff like "IF JESUS HAD HAD A GUN HE'D BE ALIVE TODAY" and "TOO COUNTRY FOR YOU" written on them. I found a monument which was a sculpture of an explorer. He had a gun and was either sleeping or dead. I think he was dead.

The nearest cathedral to us at home is called Southwark cathedral. If you don't fancy visiting that one because it's not big enough then you can go to St Paul's on the other side of the river. When I was at school I went in both of them, but I haven't been since. I suppose I should because they're iconic and everything but I keep away because I'm busy and anyway God is something made up by people who should have known better. I didn't always think this – when I was a kid I think I believed that the baby Jesus had been born in a stable and shepherds and kings of the orient came to see him with angels – but once I grew up I saw that God was bollocks. I think the thing that did it for me was when I watched a programme and they talked to this bishop who went to dinner at Buckingham Palace and sat next to a bloke from Africa. The two men had talked about the things they believed in, and the bloke from Africa told the bishop that his people believed God had made seeds, and one of the seeds had broken open and become the earth. But the earth had been dry until the God's twin had become a fish and died and been cut into hundreds of pieces, and these pieces had been sown on the dry earth and become trees and plants and flowers. And then the God had been sorry for his cut up fish twin, and brought him back to life and sent him back to earth in an ark that contained half a dozen men and half a dozen women, and they were the ancestors of all the people in the world. And the bishop who was from somewhere like Devon had laughed at this story and then smiled like Christians do when they're trying to understand or be sympathetic, and said something about the word of God and Jesus and how we live in a modern age where seeds do not become worlds. But when the bloke from Africa asked the bishop how a woman could be made from a bloke's rib and a snake could talk and why should forty two kids be killed because they laughed at a bald man and how could a virgin push a kid out, the bishop smiled and said "Faith, my son. You have to have faith." And the bloke from Africa said "I've got all the faith I need, mate," and finished his pudding. And because the dinner was in Buckingham Palace the pudding was good.

CLAIRE WITH A HARD SHELL CASE ON WEDNESDAY

I left the cathedral, decided I'd go back to see it again when it wasn't full of people taking selfies, and drove to the airport to pick up Claire. Her plane was late so I bought a bowl of leek and potato soup and a cheese and onion sandwich, and sat at a table to eat. The soup was good and the sandwich was okay, and when I'd eaten I found a place by the window where I could watch the planes. There was a very small one for people who wanted to visit the small islands to the north. Their luggage was taken out in a little trolley, and the door in the side of the plane was tiny. There was a bigger plane that flew to places like Glasgow and Edinburgh, but it wasn't going anywhere.

A television was on with the sound up. It had one of those rolling news programmes. I sat and watched for half an hour. Three people were talking about Brexit and what would happen if there was a second referendum. A woman said that since the first referendum, loads of old people who'd voted for Brexit had died and loads of young people could now vote, and lots of the people who wanted to stay in who hadn't bothered to vote the first time round because they thought they'd win anyway so what was the point, they'd vote, so the result of the second referendum would be a majority to stay in. And that would be great said the woman, but a man with glasses shook his head and went red and said there'd be riots on the streets if that happened. And I wondered where else you can have a riot. Okay, you can have one in a football ground and a prison or a factory, but you can't have a riot in a library. Not unless it was a small riot and quiet. But then my thinking was interrupted because a voice announced the arrival of the delayed plane from Aberdeen, and I got up to watch it land.

I don't usually get nervous or that weird thing you get in your stomach when you're not sure what's about to happen, but on that Wednesday afternoon at Kirkwall airport I did, and as the plane came towards the terminal and parked and its propellers stopped, I thought water would help. So I got a bottle from the shop and drank it. I'd been right. It made me feel better. So when I went back to the place where you could stand to watch people arrive, and Claire appeared, and she was carrying a bag, and she smiled when she saw me and came right over and said "Hi Ed!" I felt my heart give only the slightest jump. And my legs behaved. And I said "Hi. How was the flight?"

"Only half an hour late," she said, "so I'd call that good."

The suitcase thing that goes round started up, and we went and stood next to it. Her bag was black and one of those hard shell ones, and looked like it had seen some action. She grabbed it and when I offered to carry it she said "It's okay. I can manage…" and we strolled out of the airport to the car park.

When I'd seen her before she'd been wearing the sort of clothes you wear to an office. Smart suits, white blouses and perfect shoes. Now she was wearing jeans and a check shirt, the sort of jacket people who ride horses wear, and boots. There was a scarf around her neck and she wore little silver earrings in the shape of leaves. There were highlights in her hair that hadn't been there before. They were dark red and shone, so from the back her head looked like a conker. I took her bag and put it in the back of the van and let her climb up. I got in and started up. She was so out of my league that I didn't even bother to think about it. She reached across and patted my arm. My arm was solid and splattered with paint. Her hand was warm. Her nails were short and painted with very dark red polish. She said "Thanks so much for this, Ed."

"No worries," I said, and we headed out of the car park.

As I drove, the van filled with the scent of her. It was different to the one she'd worn when I met her in The Jam Factory. This one was less like fruit cake and more like leaves and smoke. It came in little wafts, which is what class does, I thought. It doesn't throw itself at you. It peeks out for a moment and then it pops back in again.

"Mind if I open the window?" she said.

"Go for it."

And class always asks, I thought.

"Thanks."

And says a thank you.

She let the wind blow through her hair, and after a few minutes staring said "How's it going at the house?"

"Good."

"You like it here?"

"Yeah. It's been good."

"Isn't it?" she said. "I love it." She put her hand out of the window, palm out. "Sometimes I wonder if selling the house is such a good idea."

"Really?"

"Maybe."

"But I've got rid of half the furniture."

She shrugged. "That stuff was tired anyway. No. But the house. It's a lovely place, isn't it?"

"It's great."

She looked at me and smiled. I kept my eyes on the road. We were on the edge of Kirkwall. She was still smiling. I glanced at her. I've got good teeth but hers were better. I had one at the back taken out when it grew wrong. I don't think she'd ever had any taken out.

As I drove through the middle of town I had to slow down and stop. Something had happened outside the cathedral. An ambulance was parked up and someone was lying on the pavement. I have no idea what had happened but it didn't look good. A policeman was directing the traffic. He beckoned me on. I did as I was told. I took a narrow back lane and then I was on a street I recognised, and five minutes later we were on the road to Stromness.

FAT NAKED PAGAN
WEIRDOS

As we were passing a sign that pointed towards things called the Stones of Stenness and the Ring of Brodgar, Claire asked if I'd seen any of the sights. I told her about Skara Brae and how I thought it was made up. She laughed, and when I told her that I thought the soup in the café next to the gift shop was worth the visit she laughed again. I read somewhere that if you can make a woman laugh you're one step away from having her running her fingers though her hair, and when a woman runs her fingers through her hair she's telling you that she fancies you. Yeah, and I'm a Brazilian skateboarder called Pablo, and have a major sponsorship deal with a manufacturer of hats.

"The stones are amazing," she said, "but you can't visit during the day at this time of year."

"Why not?"

She pointed. Dozens of cars and campers were in the car park, three buses were also there, and two more were leaving. "But once they've gone for their dinner it's quiet. And once the sun's gone down the only people you'll meet are naked weirdos."

"Sweet."

"Fat weirdos."

"Not so sweet."

"Fat naked pagan weirdos."

"Lovely."

I dropped her at The Ferry. She said she was going to check

in, take a shower and lie down for an hour. She'd been up since half five but didn't look it. I drove on and parked up and sat at the wheel for a moment. I'd been thinking about my adventure in the garden of the house with the plastic owl, and it bothered me. I decided to go and apologise. It's not a good idea to trample a stranger's flowers.

The lady was sitting on her lawn in a deckchair, reading a book. She put it down when I opened the gate at the bottom of the path. "Ah…" she said, "the young man who lost his boot." She looked at the bruise on my head. "How are we feeling this morning?"

I said "I just wanted to apologise for messing up your garden."

She smiled. "That's very good of you, but I think we were all young once. I know I was. And so was Alec."

"Alec?"

"My husband."

"He's in his studio." She pointed over her shoulder. "If you want to say hello, I'm sure he wouldn't mind."

"I think I should," I said.

"Just knock."

"Thanks."

I knocked. Alec came to the door. He was holding a pair of tweezers and wearing a white apron stained with flecks of paint. "Ah…" he said. "Our midnight prowler."

"I'm sorry," I said. "I just spoke to your wife, and wanted to see you too. Last night… I was trying to get home from the pub, and got lost."

"Clearly. And you're?"

"Ed."

"Ed." He offered me his hand. We shook. "Alec."

"And I hope I didn't mess up your flower beds."

"No," he said. "I don't think you did."

"If I have, let me know. I've done gardening. I'll make it good."

"I'm sure any damage is easily dealt with."

"Cool," I said.

"You're working here?"

"Yeah. At Shore View. Mr Bowen's place."

"Of course. Vic Bowen was such a good friend."

"I never met him, but I heard good things. Marcus gave me the job."

"He's a good chap too."

"He is."

From where I was standing I could see the shelves Ellen had talked about, and the bowls and some other things. Dishes and plates. Alec saw me looking. "And now I suppose you're looking for bowly."

"What?"

"Last night, as well as telling us you'd lost your boot, you said you'd lost a bowl. You called it bowly."

"Did I?"

"You did."

"Ah…"

He opened the door wider. "As you can see, we have lots of bowls, but I don't think any of them is yours. But you're welcome to look."

Alec wasn't wrong. The shelves that lined his studio were packed with bowls, dishes, plates, mugs, cups and jugs, but I didn't see one that matched the description of the one I was look- ing for. There were also china animals, glass birds, fossils, shells, and strange bent things made of metal. One shelf was stacked with empty glass bottles, and another was lined with a row of photo- graphs of sailing ships. An enormous bookcase stood at the far end of the studio, and underneath a window that looked out of the back garden, the roofs of neighbouring houses and the harbour, was a heavy workbench. This was scarred and splattered with paint and covered in tiny chisels, screwdrivers, bradawls and other miniature tools. At the back of the bench were reels of cotton and string in tall wooden holders, and pots of glue and paint. And in the middle was a small cradle, and sitting in the cradle was a model sailing ship, and next to the sailing ship was an empty bottle, and next to the empty bottle was another bottle with a ship inside it. The ship was sailing on a stormy sea, and there was an island built into the base of the bottle with a lighthouse and a tiny house.

"Wow," I said. "Wow."

"You like it?"

"It's amazing. Incredible. You made it?"

He nodded. "Here…" he picked it up and gave it to me. "She's called the Pogoria." He pointed at the little island. "That's the island of Graemsay, and the High Hoy lighthouse." It's not to scale, but it's all about perspective."

Holding the bottle made me nervous. I handed it back and said "I want a ship in a bottle."

He shook his head. "Sorry. Not for sale."

"Shame," I said. "And the rest of this stuff…"

"My collection."

"Mr Bowen had a lot of stuff like this too."

"I know. He had some fabulous pieces. I hope Marcus knows what's there."

"He does," I said. "And what's missing."

"Something's missing?"

"Yeah."

"What?"

"A bowl."

"Ah…" said Alec, and he smiled. "That wouldn't be bowly, would it?"

"I'm sorry. I was drunk."

"I know."

"And does bowly have a name? Other than bowly?"

"I don't think so. Unless she's called Lucie."

"Lucie? No…"

"Yeah."

"And would her surname be Rie?"

"Yes."

"You are joking. His Lucie Rie is missing?"

"Yeah."

"How?"

I shook my head. "It was here when Marcus came up for the funeral, but when he was here at the weekend it was gone."

"Gone? What do you mean, gone? Stolen?"

"That's what he thinks."

"But that's appalling. Have the police been informed?"

"Of course."

"And?"

"They're going to put a picture of it on their Twitter feed."

"Their what?"

"Their Twitter feed."

Alec shook his head. "Of course," he said, and he grabbed a chair and sat down. He sat down but he didn't just sit down, he crumpled into the chair as if it was a pond and he was a bird, and he started to dissolve. Or shrink. Or whatever the word is. He looked at the floor and he looked at me and then he looked out of the window at his view, the roofs and water. "Their Twitter feed…" he whispered, and he shook his head. "I don't suppose they could just ask around. I wonder if that's occurred to them? I can think of a few people who might know something."

"Do you?"

"Of course."

"Like who?"

"Well, they could start with Ellen Scott."

"Who?"

"Our cleaner. If it wasn't for Elsie thinking the best of everyone, that girl would be out on her ear. I know her type. Light fingered isn't in it. And she used to clean for Vic Bowen."

"Did she?"

"I'll bet you anything she's still got a key."

I let that thought sink in. It floated. "So tell me…"

"What?"

"If you had one of Lucie Rie's bowls, and you wanted to sell it, would that be an easy thing to do?"

Alec shook his head. "No. It would be a very difficult thing to do. Provenance is everything."

"What's provenance?"

"Evidence of where it's come from. Proof that it's real, that it's not a fake. I know for a fact that Vic had a signed invoice from Lucie Rie that described the glaze, the dimensions, the date it was fired. He showed it to me. But even if you can prove the provenance, if it's stolen, if you put it in a sale and someone spotted it… there are collectors out there who are living catalogues of her stuff."

"So if Marcus offered a reward for it, that would be a way to cash in?"

"It would. Why? Has he offered one?"

"Not yet. But he might."

Alec narrowed his eyes at me and said "Is there something

you're not telling me?"

    "Right now," I said, "I don't know."

SKIING HORSES EAT OMELETTES

I went back to Shore View. Claire wasn't there. I imagined her at The Ferry, unpacking her stuff, taking a shower, drying her hair, wrapping herself in towels, lying down, looking at the ceiling, closing her eyes, listening to a tap dripping, taking a nap and dreaming about whatever a woman like her would dream about. I don't know. What would Claire dream about?

Skiing?

Horses?

Skiing horses?

Omelettes?

I went upstairs and spent an hour being busy with a paint brush and a large pot of emulsion. As I was finishing the ceiling of the small bedroom I heard footsteps in the alley and the front door opened. A voice called. "Hello! Ed?"

"Claire?"

"Hi!"

"Up here."

She came up the stairs and I met her on the landing. She'd changed. She was wearing black jeans and a dark blue shirt, and had that polished look women get when they've had a shower. She smelt like a florist's shop on a hot day. "It's looking good," she said.

"Thanks," I said. "It's coming on."

She went into the bedroom I was sleeping in, bent down and

looked out of the window. "I love this room," she said. "When I stayed Daddy used to move into the back room and let me use it."

"I've been sleeping like a log."

"That'll be the air." She bent down and looked under the bed.

"And the quiet," I said. "Where we live gets a tad noisy."

"Where's that?"

"Bermondsey. Behind Guy's."

"Of course," she said, and "There it is," and pulled a suitcase out from under the bed. She hauled it up and said "Mother's things."

"Marcus said."

It was an old style thing, leather with big brass locks and a chunky handle. She patted it and said "I'll have a look later…" and parked it under the window.

"And you?"

"And me what?"

"Where'd you live?"

"Greenwich."

"Oh I like Greenwich."

"You know it?"

"Know it?" I said. "Of course I know it…' and I told her how when we were kids, Dad, Sally and Mum and me used to go on the bus to Greenwich Park and roll down the hill.

"I used to do that too! It was my favourite thing."

"What are your other favourite things?"

"Now you're asking…"

"Go on."

"Windy nights. Rain on a tin roof. Mark Rothko."

"Who?"

"He's a painter."

"Okay."

"Not as good as you though."

"Stop it."

"Proper tea. Decent coffee."

"You want a cup?"

"I wouldn't say no."

"You got the makings?"

"Yeah."

"Then it's coming right up," I said, and we went downstairs.

It was a warm afternoon so we took chairs to the pier and drank our coffee with the sun on our faces and seagulls winging over the water. She asked me about my work and I told her that yes, I did enjoy it, except when we had to do something like a roof in winter. I asked her about hers, and she told me. I tried to understand but it wasn't easy. She worked at Canary Wharf as a risk analyst for a company that provided trade-related credit insurance solutions to global corporations. She'd lost me by the time she was halfway through the word "insurance" but said I wasn't to worry, she wasn't going to tell me anything else about what she did. And anyway, she wasn't going to spend the rest of her life sitting at a desk in an office with a phone in one hand and a phone in the other. "I make a ton of money," she said, "but I hate the work. One day I'm going to do something different. Something that makes me happy." When I asked her what would make her happy she said "That depends on the day of the week."

"It's Wednesday," I said, "and the sun is shining."

"Oh, if it's Wednesday I'm in full-on Italian wine-maker mode."

"Thursday?"

"That depends. If it's raining I'm a baker in a little village in Cornwall. My cheese scones are to die for."

"How are your pasties?"

"Not bad…"

"I won't ask you what you'd like to be at the weekend."

"You will."

"Okay. What would you…"

"A trapeze artist."

I don't know why but I knew. I knew she'd say something like a trapeze artist. Either that or a lion tamer. Or something else in a circus though I don't think they have lion tamers in circuses anymore. Whatever. She'd surprised me and I liked her. She wasn't the woman I thought she was. She did know about clout and money but I don't think she thought they were important. Certainly not as important as doing something worthwhile, or something you enjoyed. She said "What about you? If you weren't a builder…"

"Oh that's easy. I'd be a chef. Every day of the week."

"A chef? I'd never have guessed that."

"Oh yes."

"Why?"

"I love cooking."

"Do you? What's your signature dish?"

"My signature dish? Now that does depend on the day of the week."

"Tuesday."

"You eat meat?"

"Oh yes."

"Okay. Seared beef in a sort of pesto thing with toasted pine nuts, roasted peppers on the side."

"Yum. Friday?"

"Filo fish pie."

"Tonight?"

"You want me to cook?"

"Why not?"

"Pasta?"

"Want me to do a salad?"

"Does the Pope have a balcony?"

"I don't know. Why? Can't he smoke out the window?"

She was so right.

SPAG TART

At home I cook alone. The kitchen's small and no one follows my instructions. They say I'm too bossy so they sit in front of the telly and watch programmes about driving and wait for me to put the food on the table.

I'd never cooked with anyone before but Claire anticipated, poured wine and didn't say things like "I wouldn't do it like that..." when I bashed garlic with the bottom of a glass.

I made Spaghetti alla Puttanesca which I know started as something a top chef tossed together when some of his friends rocked up late and hungry. How many of the best recipes started like this? Hundreds. And how many recipes like this are so easy to play with? Hundreds. How many recipes are called "Spag Whore"? One. And how many glasses of wine should you drink when you're cooking? At least two.

The sauce is simple – garlic, chilli, olives, capers, tomatoes, anchovies and a shot of white wine. Some people cook it one way, other people cook it another. The spaghetti is easier. You follow the instructions on the packet. Then you frig with the sauce, add some balsamic, lemon juice and basil, wet it and stir in the spag. I wasn't sure if there was enough anchovy in the sauce, but no one will tell you what they think about anchovy. Anchovy embarrasses people. So I did what I could.

"How's the salad?"

"Good."

"Ready to go?"

"You bet."

Life is a cracker of surprise. One minute you're painting a wall for a millionaire, the next you're drunk in a flower bed. Then you're staring out of a window at a blue pointy Viking, and then a woman is riffing with you about the Pope. Some days I wonder if I was born into the right world and some days I kick myself for being born. And then I get out of bed.

I scored with my Spaghetti alla Puttanesca. Claire loved it. Her salad was good too. Rocket with a dressing of her own making. Extra virgin, lemon, honey, vinegar, seasoning and the hint of something I couldn't identify.

We ate at the kitchen table. She said she remembered the table from when she was a kid. "I made those marks," she said, and she pointed at some curved scratches that had darkened into the grain. "I didn't do it on purpose, but Daddy was furious. I can't blame him. It's a lovely piece. Nan's Pembroke table. It's coming back to mine."

"Okay."

"All the stuff we didn't want has gone, right?"

"Yeah. This morning."

"And did Marcus explain where the rest of the stuff is going?"

"Not really."

"Okay. We'll do that tomorrow."

"Did he tell you…" I said, and then I stopped myself. I didn't want ruin the evening by reminding her about the missing bowl or – if she didn't already know about it – breaking the news.

"Did he tell me what?"

"That…" but I had a back up. "That I found a photograph. I think it's of you and Marcus when you were kids. On a beach. Hang on…" I got up, opened a cupboard, found it and put it on the table. "There you go."

"Ah, Charmouth! Look at us! " she said. "Where did you find it?"

"Down the back of the chest in the front bedroom."

"We were almost cute, and Mummy…" She touched the photograph. "She was so beautiful. And happy. Always happy, even when things got rough. It funny how some people can be like that, isn't it? She spent the last year of her life in terrible pain, but never let it show. She laughed at it."

"My Gran was like that. She had to have her leg amputated, but she thought it was one big joke. She used to say that even with one leg she was a better striker than Barry Kitchener."

"Who's Barry Kitchener?"

"Millwall legend, Claire, Millwall legend. Central defender, so of course one-legged Gran was a better striker than him. Mind you, on her day she was probably a better striker than Pelé. More pasta?"

"I think I will. It's superb."

"Thanks." I had a forkful of salad. "And there's something in this dressing I don't recognise."

"Yes you do."

"No I don't. What is it?"

"It's bitter. It's…"

"Coffee."

"No way."

"It makes it, doesn't it?"

"I'd never have thought. Who showed you that?"

"I picked it up in the States."

"It's great."

"Just a teaspoon."

My phone pinged with a message.

"You going to check that?"

"We have a rule in our family. No phones at the table."

"That's a good rule."

"Anyway, this time of day, I'm pretty sure who it is." I picked up my glass. "And the wine's okay? It's only from Tesco, and I don't know anything about wine."

She tapped the bottle. "Fiano. It's fine. But next time you pick up a bottle there's a shop in Kirkwall you have to visit." She took a sip from her glass. "And what the chap there doesn't know about this stuff isn't worth knowing."

"I want to find out about wine. Like, I don't know, I want to find out about birds." I think the wine was starting to go to my head. Either that or whatever.

"Birds?"

"Yeah. Oyster Catchers, Red Shanks, Curlews. I got a book."

"Well, you're in the right place."

"I know. They're everywhere. It's mental."

"They're one of the reasons Daddy moved up here. He wasn't a twitcher, but he loved watching them," she said.

"What's a twitcher?"

"You know, those people who chase after rare birds, make lists of them. They're like train spotters. You get a lot of them up here."

"Have you seen an Oyster Catcher?"

"Of course."

"They're my favourite so far."

"Are they?" Claire said.

"Yeah," I said. "I think they've got a sense of humour. At least they look like they should have," and I drank some more wine.

I don't know but I think it was when she said "Are they?" like that, in a way that was a question about Oyster Catchers and me but also a question about something more but I couldn't say exactly what, I think it was then that a switch was flicked or whatever you want to call it. Looking back I suppose I could have chosen any moment but I choose that one, and it stuck.

OBSERVATORY CREST

When the tourists are sleeping and the locals are drinking, and the divers are doing whatever divers do when they're together, and six birds are dozing in their nests, and drizzle is falling as blossom, then Stromness turns orange. The street lights glow on the slick streets, the slick streets are quiet, and there's something elusive about the world. You can't catch it. You could try but believe me, don't bother.

So we'd shared a bottle of wine and there was another to drink, and maybe I shouldn't have driven, but when Claire said the moon was rising and tonight would be a perfect night to visit the old Ring of Brodgar, I said "Let's go."

"Can you drive?"

"Easy."

"Sure about that?"

"Check it." I put my hand out. It did not tremble.

"Okay," she said.

My phone pinged again. I checked it.

"She's keen…" said Claire.

I looked at her and smiled but said nothing.

"What's her name?"

"Magda," I said, but I didn't say anything else. I was out the door, down the alley into the van and then we were driving.

I drove steady and did not crash into anything or run over anyone or cats as I drove out of Stromness to the main road, and then I was on full beam and listening while Claire told me that when her old man was alive, she had a list of things she always did when she visited, and top of that list was taking a night time drive to the stones. "You know how people say that some places are magical, and when you actually see them they're actually crap?"

"No."

"Okay, believe me Ed. If you get the Ring of Brodgar right, it really is magical."

"What do you mean, right?"

"A night like this. A big moon, still enough so you can hear the night birds and smell the grass…"

"When I was at school we went to Stonehenge. It was rubbish."

"This isn't."

The Ring of Brodgar is a big circle of stones. It's very old and quite tall. When it was made there were more stones than there are now, but over the years half of them have been nicked. No one knows why it was built or what it was used for. Some people reckon it was used to take measurements of the sun, the moon and the stars, and allowed people to work out when it was a good time to sow their crops. Other people say it was a place where ceremonies were held and animals were sacrificed. Another crowd believe it's a place where UFOs used to land, but the first two lots of people tell this lot to grow up. The pagans and/or hippies who visit the place to mix their piss in a bucket and get hitched believe it was built by a bunch of men to celebrate the oneness of the world, the beauty of nature and the importance of women going topless.

I don't know about any of this. Why couldn't it have been built simply because it looked nice, like a big rockery for people who liked to chase hairy elephants with spears? I know that clever people who know about old stuff would disagree but I'm a builder, and I've worked for dozens of people who wanted something built in their back garden because it's a 'feature' or 'just looks great there'. I've never met anyone who wanted something built because they wanted to work out when the longest day was or because they wanted to stab a virgin and drink her blood. Yeah, I know. You don't need to tell me, but that's my thinking and I'm sticking with it.

Claire's thinking had been spot on. We lucked out. As we pulled into the car park another car was leaving and then we were alone with the moonlight on the lake that was there and the quack of distant ducks. We crossed the road and went through a gate, and a wide path climbed a slope to the stones. It was laid with plastic grating so our footsteps sounded hollow in that field. There were signs that explained what was what, and pictures of what the place might have looked like when it was first built. In some of the pictures people were standing around. They were wearing animal skins and holding spears, but I didn't see any hairy elephants. Maybe they were all dead. Then there was another gate and the ground levelled off, and we could walk around the stones.

Another sign said that you were not allowed to walk into the middle of stones but it was rubbish there anyway with lots of prickly bushes and stuff, so we did as we were told and walked around the edge. When we were about a quarter of the way round we left the circle and climbed a little mound. It wasn't high but it offered a great view of all the stones, the lakes that surrounded the place, and some hills. The moon shone on the water and made the stones glow, and stars twinkled. Every now and again a bird made its sound, and then another one. They sounded like they were trapped in boxes. I said "What are they?"

"Curlews, I think."

"They're the ones with big noses."

"Beaks," she said. "Big beaks."

"Yeah," I said. "I know."

We spent an hour at the Ring of Brodgar, sometimes walking together, sometimes heading off in opposite directions. At one point I was on my own in the field that surrounded the stones and she was fifty metres away, and Claire opened her arms and tipped her head back and turned in a little circle. I didn't hear her shout but she might have done. And then she dropped her arms and ran towards the stones and disappeared. I saw her again ten minutes later, running again, and making little jumps.

I didn't run or jump, but I did sit down with my back to one of the stones, and I tried to feel whatever it is that hippies say they feel. I felt nothing but I did see a shooting star, and a moment later Claire ran up and said "Did you see it?"

"What?"

"The shooting star."

"Yeah."

"Did you make a wish?"

"I did. You?"

"Of course."

She sat down next to me and we waited for another. We waited five minutes, then ten but the stars were quiet. My phone wasn't. It pinged again. I ignored it.

"Keen and persistent," Claire said. She turned towards me. Her face was made blue in the moonlight. "Is she your girlfriend?"

"Used to be. She dumped me a couple of weeks ago but I think she wants to get back together."

"Oh yes…"

"Sounds like you know what I'm talking about."

"I do."

"Going to tell me about it?"

"Maybe," she said, "but right now I'm starting to feel a bit cold."

I stood up. "Here." I took off my jacket. She stood up. I put the jacket around her shoulders.

"Thank you, Ed. You're a gentleman."

"Yeah, right," I said.

"No, really."

"Come on," I said. "Home."

CLAIRE TALKS ABOUT
NEOLITHIC ELECTRICITY

At the house I told Claire I was an expert at lighting fires and proved it by lighting one. She said she was an expert at opening bottles of wine. I told her I was an expert at fitting kitchen work tops. She said she was an expert at analysing the credit-worthiness of energy sub-contractors. I said "Pour the wine."

We sat and drank and she asked me what I'd thought about the stones, and I told her my idea that they'd been put there because they looked good. "It was some rich bloke's garden. You know, a chief or something."

"You think it's a Neolithic rockery?"

"Could be. It's rocks."

"They're stones."

"Stones, rocks, whatever. What about you?"

"I think people used to worship whatever they worshipped, the sun, the moon, the earth. And I think it was live once, you know, like a electrical socket, and people used to go along and sort of plug themselves into it. But it's switched off now. Dead…

I had wine. "Maybe…"

"When you put your hand on one of the stones, I think you should be able to feel something. I don't know, a current, a pulse…"

"Okay…"

"Oh God."

"What?"

"Roll me a joint. I'm sounding like a hippy."

"Not really. And you don't look like a hippy."

"I don't feel like a hippy."

"Okay," I said. "You're not a hippy."

"Pass the bottle."

"There you go."

She poured some more wine and drank. We stared at the fire, and the fire crackled.

"You were going to tell me something."

"Was I?"

"When I was telling you about Magda dumping me."

She shook her head. "I think I said 'maybe'".

"Yeah, but…"

"I've been going out with this guy for a couple for years. Anthony. Works in corporate finance. Typical city boy, if you know what I mean. Do you know what I mean?"

"I think so…"

"Rich, clever but a bit thick. Very nice, polite all that, but there's something missing. I don't know what, but something. It's like he's incomplete. Everyone says I'm lucky, and I know we've got a lot in common, but it's the things we don't have in common that bother me."

"Tell me about it."

"I mean, rugby. He's fanatical about it. He supports Harlequins. The night before a match he wears his scarf to bed, like a little boy. I laughed at him when I first saw that. And that was the first time we split up. He wasn't happy…"

"And the second time?"

"Because I wanted to go to a concert at the Festival Hall, but it clashed with this dinner he wanted to take me to. Not a romantic dinner for two, mind, it was a corporate bash where the chaps show off their women and if you don't wear heels people think something's wrong with you. You know the sort of thing…"

"No," I said, "I don't. I'm a builder."

"Well you're not missing anything," she said.

"And you're back together?"

She shook her head. "No. We split again a couple of weeks ago. I don't know. I think I'm too old for it."

"What's it?"

"Splitting up and getting back together. It's what you do when you're seventeen, not when you're thirty."

"People do it at any age."

"That's what scares me, Ed. I don't want to. I hate the drama. The angriness. The angry texts. The nasty emails…"

"I know."

"I want the sort of thing my Mum and Dad had."

"It was good?"

"Very good," she said, and she yawned. "I'm sorry. I need my bed."

"Me too."

She stood up, necked the last of her wine and went through to the kitchen. I followed. "I've been thinking," she said. "Tomorrow."

"What about it?"

"Fancy the day off?"

"I don't know. It depends. Does a day off mean I drop my wages?"

"Full pay, all meals included."

"What you planning?"

"I promised I'd visit an old friend of Daddy's. He lives on one of the islands, but I'll need wheels."

"Okay."

"We'd have to take a ferry."

"How big is it?"

"Eday?"

"What's Eday?"

"The island."

"No, the ferry."

"I don't know. Medium size. Why?"

"Nothing," I said. "Okay."

"It'll be an early start."

"How early?"

"We'd have to be out of here at six. The ferry's at seven."

"You got it."

She opened the door and stepped into the alley.

"I'm glad you're coming," she said.

"Why?"

"Because I booked the van onto the ferry this morning. And I can't drive."

"Right..." I said. "Fine."

"Are you cross with me?"

"Why would I be cross with you?"

"Because I just assumed you'd drop everything and drive me. That's one of the things Anthony says is annoying about me. Making assumptions..."

"Assume all you like, Claire. Doesn't bother me. As long as you're paying, I'll do what you want."

"Oh yes?"

"Yeah."

"I'll bear that in mind."

"Want me to walk you back?"

She took another step. "I think I'll be okay."

I said "Thanks for showing me the stones."

"And thank you for the pasta. It was delicious."

"The salad made it," I said.

"Oh stop it," she said, and she leant forward and kissed me on the cheek.

"Tomorrow, six," she said, and then she turned and walked away, and I watched her until she was around the corner and the sound of her boots had faded.

I CANNOT BE TAKEN
ANYWHERE, NOWHERE

I knew I would because I always do, and I dreamt about Claire. She was beautiful and I was with her and we were students of architecture. We were visiting a modern building. Looking at the building was part of our course. We stood outside and pointed at the windows and then we went inside and looked at the walls. We were wearing soft shoes and pale hats because we had to. The building had lots of doors and was made of very smooth concrete. Although people had said it was ugly and had written about it in newspapers I thought it was beautiful, and when I asked Claire what she thought about the place she said "It's mine".

An orchestra was playing upstairs. They were playing gentle and twiddly classical music, and in the dream I thought to myself that it was time I learnt about classical music because it sounds like food tastes. I opened and closed some doors but this wasn't a good idea because it disturbed the people who were listening to the music. A woman came towards us. She was a long way away. I knew she was coming to tell me off for closing the doors loudly. We got out of the building and closed the last door before the woman reached us, and then we were in a street and Claire said to me "I can't take you anywhere".

"Yes you can," I said. "Take me to dinner."

"Dinner?"

"Now."

"Now?"

"Yeah."

"Okay."

So she took me to a restaurant that had its own weather. You could sit at a table and the menu started with a list of different types of weather. There was warm and sunny, tropical thunderstorm, blizzardy snow, autumnal wind, London fog and a couple of others. We chose autumnal wind, so as we ate our meal leaves swirled around our hands and feet, the sound of migrating geese filled the air, and everything smelled of bonfire smoke. The food was good too. Claire had venison and I had a piece of fish, and I ate it carefully.

As we were leaving I said "You can take me anywhere."

"Yes," her voice said, but when I turned to look at her she wasn't there.

I woke up for a few minutes and sat up. I looked down at the orange light on the harbour water. I lay back down again. I could hear a sort of whispering noise outside. I got up and looked out of the window. I couldn't see anyone, just a bunch of ducks on the water. I went back to bed. The whispering carried on. I listened to it and didn't go back to sleep for at least an hour.

PEOPLE WHO SOUND OR
LOOK LIKE SAUSAGE

Claire knocked on the door at six. I'd been in the shower. I was wearing a towel and smelt of soap. I apologised. She'd been up for ages. She was pink and fresh. I felt rough. I apologised again, went upstairs and got dressed. While I was doing that, she fetched one of her father's paintings from the living room and wrapped it in newspaper. "A present for Hermann," she said. Hermann was the bloke we were going to visit on Eday.

We were on the road by ten past. We didn't talk much, and when we reached Kirkwall and the place where the ferries left, we queued up and closed our eyes for ten minutes. Other people in the queue did the same thing. The world smelled of diesel and fish. I got that wired feeling you get when you haven't slept enough and haven't had your breakfast. I was wondering if I'd have time to fetch a cup of coffee from somewhere when a man in hi-vis knocked on the window and told us we could drive on to the ferry.

I hadn't told Claire how I felt about boats. I hadn't told Claire a lot of things about myself like for example the time I had a three-some with nurses even though she probably wouldn't have cared. And I hadn't told her what I felt about her and how the scent of her perfume in the van made me feel dizzy but in a good way, and I still hadn't said anything about her bowl. I suppose you could say I was a big ball of confusion, but I worked hard to look cool as I followed another van onto the ferry and parked where I was told to park. Then I did what a sign told me to do. I applied the handbrake, vacated the vehicle and followed Claire into the boat.

We went upstairs. There was a lounge there and doors to the outside. We went and stood at some railings. On one side we could look down and watch the last few cars driving on, and on the other side we could look down and see the sea though I wasn't sure if it was the sea. Was it just the harbour? For where does the sea start, and where does the sea stop and become the ocean? And what about the other bits of the sea, things like straits, channels and basins. And what about coasts? There's a programme on the telly called COAST that I've seen. It's got a hippy, a bloke with an umbrella and a woman with a very long name that sounds like a Polish sausage. Claire didn't sound like a sausage but she smelt as good as one.

The ferry left bang on time. It was blue and white with red funnels, and as we went out of the harbour we passed two cruise ships. One was tied up to a pier and the other was anchored on its own in the middle of the sea. We passed close to this one, and I could see people on the decks. Some of them were jogging but most of them were walking.

The ferry was named after Earl Thorfinn who was a fearsome bloke with a sword who once ruled Orkney and lorded over plenty of other land. He lived hundreds of years ago, way before the invention of bacon rolls. I mention bacon rolls because someone came on the loudspeakers to say the cafeteria was open and I was down there in a shot, and bacon rolls were on the menu. I got three for myself, one for Claire and two cups of instant coffee. The rolls were good, and I had mine with tomato ketchup. Claire had hers without.

We spent most of the time on the ferry sitting on a bench that was set up in a part of the boat that was outside but under cover, so we had a great view of the sea, the fishing boats we passed and a few tiny islands. Some of these had seals on them. Others had loads of birds. The seals looked like they couldn't give a toss. They were lying about staring at nothing, and were overweight. I suppose no one had told the seals they should cut down on cheese.

A couple of years ago, when I went to see the doctor about the screwdriver I'd stuck in the back of my hand, and he gave me important news about the amount I drink, he said if I wanted he could give me a proper check-up. Then he said he'd have to take some blood and although I don't like needles I thought that as I'd had a screwdriver in the back of my hand a needle would be nothing so I said "Go for it" and he took some blood out of my elbow. A week later I went back to see him and he told me I was in good shape but my cholesterol was a tad high, so I should think about cutting back on stuff like butter and cheese. I told him I'd drop the butter but cheese? Forget it. Okay, so it's solid fat but I'm solid muscle unlike the seals of Orkney, who are solid fat.

We were well away from Kirkwall and the sea suddenly got rough, then went calm again. I fetched two more cups of coffee and another bacon roll and asked Claire about Hermann. She said he was a sculptor. I told her I'd done a job for a sculptor in Black-heath. She said Hermann was a bit German and very old school, and made most of his sculptures out of steel, though he also made smaller pieces out of wood and stuff he found on the beach.

"Have you heard of David Smith?" she said.

I said "Who does he play for?"

"David Smith was an American sculptor. An abstract expressionist."

"Okay."

"When Hermann was a kid he worked for Smith in Italy. The genius rubbed off."

"So he's famous?"

"Hermann's more than famous, Ed. He's an icon."

"So he sells his stuff?"

"Don't call his work 'stuff' Ed. And yes. He does. For hundreds of thousands," she said, which made me think about the stolen bowl, and when I thought about the stolen bowl I felt guilty and I don't like feeling guilty, but I still didn't say anything. I didn't want to spoil the day which was bright and blue and warming up nicely.

The ferry had been going for about an hour when it got close to Eday and we could see the fields and farms and houses of the island. There were cows and sheep in the fields, and tractors. No one waved. We started to slow down and someone came on the speakers and said that anyone who wanted to get off should go to the car deck. Drivers could get into their vehicles but anyone else had to wait. Everyone did as they were told, and ten minutes later the ferry was tied up and we were driving off. Some people were waiting to meet other people, and some cars were waiting to drive on. I drove carefully. The road curved away from the pier. There were some shipping containers there, and pens where farm animals could wait. Then the road climbed a hill to a junction. I turned right at the junction, and drove on.

RANDOM MINTED
LUMPS OF METAL

Claire told me about Eday. More people drink in The Miller on a Tuesday night than live on the island. There were some farmers there, and a few people who worked at a place that was making energy out of tides. There were wind turbines, ruined houses, places where peat used to be cut and abandoned cars in the middle of fields. There was a shop. There was a fish farm with salmon. There were a few retired people, and a big old stone that looked like a giant's hand. There were middle aged people living in huts and kids living in caravans. There was an airport called London airport because in an old language Lundi are puffins and there used to be lots of puffins on Eday, which is why Lundy off the coast of Devon is called Lundy. I got a tad lost there, but Claire told me not to worry.

"Where's the pub?" I said.

"There isn't one."

"No way."

"They make their own entertainment," she said.

"And what sort of entertainment is that?"

"I don't know."

The school had half a dozen kids, the hedgehog population was booming and if you liked birds you could see some freaky things. The lake by the shop was a good place to listen to the ghost wail of red-throated divers, and fence posts were good for spotting a type of owl that had a face like a bored cat. And if you climbed to the high ground when the skuas were nesting they'd kill you with their beaks which were bigger than their heads.

Hermann's house overlooked the sea or ocean. We parked next to a Range Rover that had seen better days. One of its windows had been replaced with lengths of laminate flooring, and the off-side back light cluster was hanging from its housing. There was a knackered garden in front of the house, which was small and low and the colour of disappointment. There was a lawn to one side of the house and a big shed at the back. This was made of corrugated iron, wood and some cement blocks. It looked like it had been in a fight with another shed. Someone was inside, hammering something. Claire grabbed the newspaper wrapped picture, jumped out of the van, strolled towards the shed and called out "Hermann!" The hammering stopped.

"Who is there?"

"Claire, Hermann…"

A door opened and a short man in a long leather apron stepped out. He had what I thought was a hat on his bald head, but it turned out to be a smudge of soot and/or black paint. "Claire? Is this Claire Bowen?"

"Yes, Hermann."

"And she's come all this way to see me?"

"She has."

"Oh joy!"

He stepped back inside his workshop and reappeared a moment later wiping his hands on a cloth that was dirtier than his hands. "Sweet Claire," he said, and he opened his arms and hugged her and kissed her on both cheeks. When he stepped away she had soot on her face. "And who is this?" he said, looking at me.

"Hi," I said. "Ed."

"Edward?"

"Yeah, but no one calls me that."

"I shall," said Hermann. "And you are the boyfriend?"

"No," I said. "I don't think so. I'm the…"

"You don't think so? Either you are or you're not…"

"I'm not," I said. "I'm a builder."

"A builder?" He turned to Claire. "You're going with a builder?"

She shrugged.

I said "I'm doing some work on her house."

"Not ruining it, I hope."

"No. Just a freshen up."

"Good." He turned back to Claire. She'd wiped most of the soot off her face, but some was still there. "And your timing is perfect. Coffee will be served in the house. Please…" and he spread his arms.

I had never been in a house like it. You walked through a door into a sort of lean-to with a washing machine and a freezer and some cupboards that had been sprayed in swirls of gold and silver paint. Small hand tools were scattered around, and random pieces of metal, and a blacksmith's anvil stood in one corner. Another door led to a bathroom, and a third opened into a large room that was half kitchen, half sitting room. The shelves in the kitchen area were lined with jars of spice and herbs, and condiments and oils and dried beans and pulses. Saucepans and skillets hung from hooks over the sink, wooden spoons were stuck in a jam jar and bowls of fruit and vegetables were on the side. Something was simmering in the oven, and it smelt good. There was a small island where you could prep, a loaf of homemade bread on a board, and an old fashioned set of scales on top of a big wooden box.

The boundary between the kitchen and the sitting area was marked by a sofa that was pushed up against the island, and the walls were covered in photographs, paintings and maps. A model aeroplane hung from the ceiling, and an old fashioned candelabra set with burned candles. The floor was covered in an old rug and there were three tables – one was pushed against a window and had a view of the sea or ocean and another island. There was an old fashioned typewriter on this table, a stack of plain paper and a mug of pencils and pens. The second table was low and small, and covered in fossils, glass balls, carved wooden things that looked like trees but weren't, and a metal toy car pulling a metal toy caravan. The third table was covered in sheets of paper torn from a sketch book, squares of canvas, more lumps of metal and a plate with a half eaten piece of toast on it. There was an open fire at the far end of the room with a comfy chair either side and more stuff on the mantelpiece. Small sculptures of women wearing not a lot of clothes, mostly. Books were stacked on the floor and on shelves, and on a couple of dining chairs.

Hermann cleared some space on the sofa, told us to make ourselves comfortable and said "You'll stay for lunch". This wasn't a question. This was what was happening.

Claire said "We'd love to, wouldn't we Ed?"

"If we're eating what I can smell then I'm not going anywhere."

Hermann smiled and said "Hasenpfeffer's cooking."

"What's that?"

"German rabbit stew."

"Nice one."

"You've had hasenpfeffer before?"

"No."

"But you've heard of it?"

"Never."

"You cook?"

"Oh yeah."

"Then the recipe will be yours."

"And this," Claire said, and she put her hand on Hermann's arm, "will be yours," and she gave him her father's picture.

"A present? Oh my. I haven't had a present for so long!" He started tearing the newspaper away. "And beautifully wrapped… and oh…" he looked at the picture. It was a small scene of clouds and sea and a distant island, or maybe it was a boat or a big wave. "Dear Vic…" he reached out for Claire and kissed her. "He was more of an artist than he knew. Truly. And such a kind man. And you're such a kind, kind woman. Thank you."

"I know he would have wanted you to have one."

"I already have three!" he said. "But this is already my favourite. The things he could do with greys." A tear had popped into the corner of his eye. "And that little touch of blue…"

"He lived here long enough."

"True. Very true." He propped the painting on a shelf and stood back to admire it. "I miss him. I miss his laugh. He had such a German laugh, you know?" and Hermann laughed, as if maybe he could conjure his friend from the ground.

And so we sat for an hour and drank coffee and Claire and he talked about the old days. I kept quiet mostly, and when Hermann said he had some work to finish and maybe we'd like to go for a walk and come back in time for lunch, it was agreed. He got up and looked out of the window. "The tide's low. Take him to the beach."

"Good plan."

"But of course."

THE SANDS OF DOOMY

We left Hermann to do whatever art he had to do, drove north and then west, parked up and walked down to a beach. There was no one else there and no footprints. The sun was bright and warm and the sea was blue and flat. There were too many birds to count. Some were oyster catchers and there were some small plump ones with brown backs and white bellies that looked like clockwork toys. They zig-zagged with the waves and never got their feet wet, pecked in the sand for things to eat and zig-zagged again. There were three of them, and they tried to stay almost exactly the same distance away from us – if we got too close they took off and flew for a bit, then dropped down and carried on with their zig-zagging. They made high cheeping sounds. I asked Claire what they were and she said "Sanderlings".

I said "They're clever."

She said "The girl birds have two boys at the same time."

I laughed at that and said "With all that running and everything else, their little hearts must have to work so fast."

Claire stopped walking, looked at me and said "I'm sorry? What?"

"Their little hearts must have to work so fast."

"I thought that's what you said," she said, and she smiled at me. She held my gaze for a moment and then she walked on.

The first bit of the beach was rocky and backed by low, crumbly cliffs. Gulls were nesting on ledges in the cliffs but they weren't gulls, they were fulmars. They were mostly grey and didn't make any noise or cries, and once they were in the air they didn't beat their wings very much, they just glided. And then there were these bright white birds who were flying a few metres from where the waves met the sand, and they flew in a very relaxed and flappy way, and every now and again they'd stall in mid-air and dive down and fold their wings at the last minute and hit the water and catch a fish. They were called terns.

A couple of curious seals were in the sea. They followed us and looked at us, their fat heads poking out of the water and looking around. I watched them and looked at the birds as I walked. Claire looked at the ground as she walked, mostly. She stopped every now and again and poked around and picked up a stone or a shell and put it in her pocket. She also looked at the birds because it was her job to tell me what they were called. I said "I should have bought my book," but she said, "You'll remember them better if I tell you."

After a few hundred yards we reached a place where slabs of rock had fallen down from the cliff, and we had to clamber. Then we were on the most beautiful part of the beach, a wide sweep called the Sands of Doomy. There were dunes with wavy grasses, and the sun shone on pools of shallow water. There were more sanderlings here, and more terns. Claire took her boots and socks off, left them on a rock, rolled up her jeans and ran towards the sea. She jumped when she reached the water, and screamed "Cold!"

"I'll bet."

"Get 'em off then."

"No chance," I said. "I don't do paddling."

"Chicken."

"Yeah, right. No one calls me chicken."

"Then get 'em off."

"No."

I let her do her paddling and I did my walking, and I did a bit of jogging but I prefer to walk because I like my knees, so that's what I did. And when I was nearly at the end of the beach I sat down on the slope of a dune and stared at the sand and the sea, and listened to the birds and the wavy grass, and I watched Claire. She did that thing where you run and kick the sea and it showers up, and then she did the twisting arms out thing she'd done at the Ring of Brodgar, and then she went back to just walking along in the water, and staring at it, and the seals stared back at her, and I can't blame them for doing that. She looked happy and beautiful like she was in a painting, and I was in some sort of gallery where you don't have to pay but you can leave some shrapnel in a big plastic box if you like the pictures.

I lay down and stared up at the sky. There weren't many clouds but there were some. They were those faint wispy ones. I wondered what they were called and how high they were. It was impossible to tell. Half a mile? A mile? Two miles? I didn't know. I saw a high plane. It was flying north. It would have been about six miles high. I know that is true because once I was worried about how you breathe in an aeroplane so I searched it.

A bird flew over me, and then another. I didn't know what sort they were. The sound of the waves on the sand was soft. Just listening to it made me feel sleepy. I suppose it was a bit like hypnotism. I closed my eyes and saw those white things you see when you close your eyes on a bright day. I counted about ten of them then stopped because it wasn't a very interesting thing to do.

My eyes were closed for about a minute. I heard a scream. I opened my eyes and sat up. Claire was running up the sand towards me. I thought something was wrong. I thought she had been attacked by a sea monster or thing from the sky but she was fine. She was just happy. When she got to where I was lying she threw herself down next to me and thrashed her legs up and down like a kid would and she yelled "Does it get any better?"

I was cool. I said "I don't think it does."

She turned towards me and I looked at her. She was a woman who knew about money and credit insurance, and she knew what the inside of an airport executive lounge looked like. She could relax but even when she did she'd still be thinking about global solutions, and I think I was waiting for her to say something serious about international stuff but she kissed me on my mouth instead, and not just the sort of kiss you might plant when you say hello but a hard one. It was meant and I was happy to mean it too, and then we had our arms around each other too, and I was folding her into me like I was a perfectly done omelette and she was the tomato and fines herbes the chef had just sprinkled and now he was getting his spatula.

The kiss didn't last for more than half a minute but it felt like ten, and when we broke she said "I…"

I said "Don't…" and put a finger on her lips.

"No," she said, and we sat there. We sat there and stared out and not at each other but it wasn't awkward. I felt it and she felt it. I knew the delight of the place had taken her and I knew the delight of the place had made me sing. And even though her perfume had made me spin since the day I met her, and I had no idea what she thought about me, I had seen her looking at my arms, and we were adult people. We had choices. We were responsible. So when I stood up and walked towards the sea she stood up too, and when I turned to look at her and she was smiling I nodded, and we didn't need to say anything.

We did say a few things as we walked back along the Sands of Doomy to the van, things like "that's a good stick…" and "I'd like to be a bird…" but the words didn't mean a lot for a door had been opened and we'd stepped through and there was no going back to the place we'd been before because the door led to a garden, and in the garden were the flowers she wanted and some interesting vegetables I could pick and clean and cook. And there was a tumbled down shed in the corner of the garden. And there was a sofa in this shed with its stuffing bursting out, and a little fireplace in the corner with a kettle hanging from a hook. And then the door closed behind us and the garden faded and we were walking along a sandy beach on an island in Orkney again, and she said "My little heart has to work so fast…" and we didn't need to hold hands again because we knew our hands were there, and if we wanted them we could have them.

HERMANN LAUTENSCHLÄGER'S HASENPFEFFER SCHLÄGT ES

To make hasenpfeffer, first you run for a few miles and catch your hase, which is German for hare. If you can't catch a hare then you catch a rabbit. That's not a difficult thing to do on Eday though you'd probably need a gun. Rabbits love the island. We saw loads but we didn't see any hares. We didn't see any squirrels either. I don't think there are enough trees on Eday for squirrels, but we did see a few bushes.

This is what Hermann told me – take your rabbit and/or hare, gut it, skin it, wash it, joint it and steep the meat in a marinade of red wine, vinegar, salt, rosemary, crushed juniper berry, black peppercorn, bay leaf, thyme and shallots. If you can't get shallots use white onion. If you can't get white onions, use red. The quality of the wine is not important, but the length of time the meat marinates is. Give it four days. During this time you can occupy yourself in a number of different ways, but I suppose most people just get on with their usual lives.

After the four days, remove the meat from the marinade, dredge it (the meat) in plain white flour, toss it into a casserole, cook the lot in a fist of butter until it's brown and then put it on a decorated plate to rest. Cook some onions in the casserole, adding more butter if you're in love. When the onions are as soft as a petal's nipple, put the meat back in the pot and add the (strained) marinade. Put the pot in a cracking oven and let the lot simmer for at least two hours. Then remove, spoon off a cup of the sauce and mix it with a dob of soured cream. Return this mixture to the pot and give it a swirl. Serve immediately.

Hermann served his hasenpfeffer with braised carrots and nutmeg flavoured semolina dumplings. He had cleared one of the tables and moved it into the middle of the room, and although it was the middle of the day, he'd lit a candle.

Claire had been quiet as I drove back from the beach but once she was sat down and the food was served and beer was poured and Hermann was asking her questions, she got talkative. He was good at getting stuff out of her, and I learnt more in a couple of hours in that house on Eday than I'd learnt in a couple of days in Stromness. I found out that although she was a top risk analyst, spoke three languages, was allergic to strawberries and could see miles from her office window, she had studied music at university, and was brilliant at the violin.

"Do you still play with your old friends?"

"Afraid not, Hermann."

"You might not know this, Edward, but Claire was a member of the finest Klezmer band I ever heard, and if anyone knows about Klezmer, that's me. You know what Klezmer is, Edward?"

"No."

"Jewish music. We play it at weddings and when we're happy, don't we Claire?"

"And sometimes when we're sad," said Claire.

"Of course."

"But when you played, how could anyone be sad?"

"A few people blocked their ears."

"Modest, beautiful, clever – what more could you want in a woman, Edward?"

"Oh do hush, Hermann."

"This stew," I said, "is delicious."

"Hasenpfeffer, Edward, hasenpfeffer."

"Sorry. And I've never had a dumpling like this."

"My grandmother's recipe. All the way from Recklinghausen. You've heard of Recklinghausen, Edward?"

"No."

"It's a fine town. They have a Henry Moore in the Ruhrfestspielhaus. You have to see him."

Again, lost, feeling stupid, and I didn't know what was going on. I had too much to learn. I wanted to get up, go to the van and drive to the ferry. But the ferry wasn't there. It wasn't coming for a few hours. But Claire was there and she smiled at me. I stayed where I was and said "Who's Henry Moore?"

Hermann's eyes widened and I think he was about to tell me that I should know who Henry Moore was, but Claire slapped the back of his hand and said "He was a grumpy old man who made sculptures, wasn't he, Hermann?"

Hermann picked up his beer. He looked at it. He might have been old but he could still be stupid. He drank and said "He was."

"And I wonder if Henry Moore ever met Barry Kitchener." Claire winked at me.

"Who is Barry Kitchener?"

"Barry Kitchener," she said, "was a Millwall legend."

"And what is Millwall?"

"Millwall," I said, "is the greatest football club in England."

"Ah…" said Hermann. "Football. I don't watch football. Not since you cheated in 1966."

"We cheated?"

"Boys…"

And so the lunch went. Hermann and I sparred, Claire and

Hermann did that thing old men and younger women do when they know they could have had something but time worked against them, and Claire and I danced without moving. When we spoke to each other we did it normally, and we gave nothing away. We were good actors.

The talk went from London to music to food and old friends, and from birds to the island. The hasenpfeffer and dumplings were good, and the beer was German. When we'd finished and the plates were cleared away, I could have easily had a nap but Hermann wanted to show us what he was working on, so we followed him to his shed. There was welding equipment there and a heavy, dark work bench covered in a load of metal objects. They were all about a foot tall, and made from angular pieces of half polished steel, welded together to create things that looked like a cross between people and machines. Or people and birds. It was difficult to tell. Whatever, I think they were clever. Hermann picked one up. The bottom shape was a rectangle, then there were a pair of triangles and a circle welded at crazy angles to each other, and another triangle on the top. The whole lot stood on a circle. A load of irregular holes had been drilled in all the shapes, like the holes in Emmental. The welds were rough but I think they were meant to be. "Here," he said, and he gave it to Claire. "For you."

"Oh Hermann. I couldn't. No way…"

"Yes you could. And you will."

"But…"

"No buts. Take her. Find her a good home."

She stroked the edge of one of the triangles and pressed it to her chest. "Thank you…" she said. "She'll have pride of place."

"Now don't embarrass me."

"Embarrass you? Would that be possible?" She put the sculpture back on the workbench, opened her arms and hugged the man.

"Now I am embarrassed," he said, and there were tears in his eyes, but I think that was because it was cold in that shed.

We spent half an hour walking around Hermann's garden. He showed us his poly tunnel. It was full of flowers and the flowers were full of bees. He showed us his rhubarb and said "I think rhubarb is God's way of telling us he hates us…" and he showed us a marshy field where he said "the ghosts of chickens live". Then he said he needed a nap, because without a nap he couldn't do any work in the evening, and the evening was the best time for him.

"We'll go and see the Stone of Setter," Claire said. The Stone of Setter was the stone that looked like a giant's hand.

"Come and say goodbye before you leave."

"Of course."

MUTTLEY OUT OF
WACKY RACES

I drove. Claire held Hermann's sculpture. She turned it over and rubbed its edges. She said "I can't believe he gave this to me."

"You gave him one of your Dad's."

"His paintings were amateur. They're worth nothing. Hermann's in Tate Modern. This is worth a fortune."

"Maybe he doesn't care what it's worth. Maybe all he cares about is his art."

"Maybe…"

"Or maybe he loves you."

She laughed at that. "I doubt that, Ed, I doubt that very much." She pointed. "Left here, pull up on the right."

The Stone of Setter stood on its own in a field. A sign pointed the way and a neat path had been mown through the grass. The stone did look like a giant's hand if the giant had been careless and left it in a giant sandwich press for an hour or so, but the most amazing thing about it was the stuff called lichen that covered it. I searched lichen later, and it turns out that without lichen you wouldn't have soil. Lichen's three organisms in one – algae, fungus and bacteria – and hundreds of millions of years ago lichen colonised the earth, grew all over rocks and helped to break the rocks down and release good stuff into the ground. And when they get the chance and clean air to breath, lichens are still being prehistoric on things like the Stone of Setter and in woods.

There were lots of different kinds of lichen on the Stone of Setter. Some were large and curly and some were small and flat, but they were all doing the same thing, and if you had good enough ears you'd be able to hear them doing it. Claire put her hand on a place where no lichen grew and closed her eyes. I went to a picnic table that stood in the corner of the field and took a picture. Claire stepped away and started to walk towards a building that stood a little way away. When I caught up with her she said "There's an old tomb up there". She pointed towards a bump on the hill. "Want to have a look?"

"Let's do it."

There were sheep on the hill, and we met a farmer and her dog. The dog was pleased to see us, and came running over. When the farmer whistled and the dog went back to doing whatever he had to do with the sheep, I said "Did I tell you about Barney?"

"Who's Barney?"

"Our dog."

"You never told me you had a dog. What sort?"

"I don't know. A bit of this, a bit of that. He was a rescue. Looks like Muttley."

"Muttley? Out of Wacky Races?"

"Yeah. Except he doesn't wear flying goggles. But he'll bite your arse. When Dad and I are working he guards the van."

"I want to meet Barney."

"That'll be up to him."

"Choosy, is he?"

"Oh yeah," I said.

The hill got steeper and we had to scramble, and we scared a sheep the farmer's dog had missed. It did a skippy thing and disappeared behind a scrubby shrub, and then the ground flattened out and the path was clear.

The tomb was a fat mound of earth. There was an entrance made of stones, and a metal gate opened into a low, narrow tunnel.

You had to crawl on your hands and knees. I thought I might get jammed. Claire said "Go first and if you get stuck I'll push you."

"You sure about that?"

"Get in."

I did as I was told.

At the end of the tunnel you could stand up. Someone had dug a hole in the roof of the tomb and fitted a clear plastic dome over the hole so it was quite light in there and you could see the little chambers where dead bodies had been laid out. It was spooky and weird to be there. I didn't like it. Okay, so the people who'd been buried there had died thousands of years ago and now their bones were dust but I felt them in that place, whispering a language I didn't understand or want to, and they had been people. They had chased hairy elephants and been mums and dads, and I felt I was intruding.

I said "I think I'll wait outside."

"Okay," she said.

I waited on top of the tomb. There was a great view of other islands from there. Some of them were big and others were small, and from that distance they all looked like gardens in the sea. I saw a bird with a beak like a hook, and I saw more sheep, and a tractor with a tall machine attached to its side. It was cutting grass and the grass was shooting out of the top of the tall machine and into a trailer that was being towed by another tractor. And then Claire appeared from the entrance of the tomb, stood up and said "Chilly…" She looked at me and I looked at her and I said "That was weird."

"Nothing like a bit of weirdness to make you realise what you're missing."

"Eh?"

She climbed the side of the tomb and said "There's nothing

like a bit of weirdness…"

"Yeah, I heard that bit. I just didn't understand what you meant."

"Well, you know how it is. You get on with your life, you go to work in the morning, you go home in the evening, you might meet someone for a drink, you might not. You watch some telly, you go to bed, you get up again…." She shaded her eyes from the sun. "You go to work in the morning…"

"Is that your life?"

"Sometimes, Ed, yes," and she gave me a long serious look. It was a look that meant something but I had no idea what. Unfinished business was hovering over us, things that needed to be said but couldn't be because we weren't sure what had to be said or whether those things were even worth saying.

I said "My life's pretty boring too, but I've worked out a few ways to liven it up."

"And how do you do that? Or should I ask?"

"I like to stick screwdrivers into the back of my hand."

"Really?"

"Yeah. Look." I showed her my hand. There was a scar there, and little white spots where the stiches had been.

"My God."

"Was that a screwdriver?"

"Yeah."

She took my hand and rubbed the scar with her finger tips. "Does it hurt?"

"Only when it's cold."

"But you didn't do it on purpose…"

"Claire."

"What?"

"I might be an idiot, but I'm not a fool."

"You…" she said, and she pulled my hand to her mouth and kissed the scar, and then she held my hand against her cheek and closed her eyes. "Are you an idiot?"

"Mostly," I said.

"That's not what I think."

"And what do you think?"

"I think," she said, and she let my hand drop but did not stop holding it, and we started to walk back the way we'd come, "that we're going to miss the ferry."

PHYSICS, MONKS AND TITS

We didn't miss the ferry. We had plenty of time so we called in at the shop and I bought a bar of chocolate and postcard with a picture of the Stone of Setter, and we stopped to say goodbye to Hermann. He was in his shed in full welding kit. "I'm sorry," he said, "but I have the flow. And I don't do goodbyes. So go well…" and he waved us off and went back to work. We drove down to the pier, queued up and waited for ten minutes.

When we'd caught the ferry from Kirkwall we'd driven on at the back of the boat but now, as it approached Eday, its front opened up like a big mouth. When it started to do this I said "Oh fuck…"

"What's the matter?"

"I'm sorry, but I've got a thing about boats. I wasn't going to tell you, but that…" I pointed at the front going up… "That's just wrong."

"You've got a thing?"

"Yeah."

"What sort of thing?"

Now I was embarrassed but it was too late to turn back. "Well, I know they're not going to sink or anything like that, but they're so heavy and I just can't get my head around the fact that they don't."

"They don't what?"

"Sink."

"Okay…"

"Because when you put a nail in the bath, it sinks doesn't it?"

"I've never put a nail in the bath, but yes, I suppose it does…"

"So why doesn't that?" I pointed at the ferry.

She had a think. "Because it's buoyant?"

"But what's that?"

"It's, er, I don't know. Air? Something to do with the ferry having lots of air in it?"

"The ferry's got lots of air in it? That's comforting."

"I have no idea, Ed. Really. I'm not a physicist. I was useless at that sort of thing. I do money…" but then the conversation ended because a bloke asked me to drive onto the ferry, which is what I did. And once again, I did as I was told and parked in a tight spot and turned the engine off and we went to find a place to sit.

The journey back to Kirkwall was better than the one we'd done in the morning. The sea was smoother and the sun was at an angle in the sky that made the light gold and mauve and orange and pink and other colours I don't know the names of. We talked about what it would be like to live in a place like Eday and wondered what winter was like there, and we saw some small black birds with white patches on their wings that turned out to be black guillemots, and are common in Orkney.

I went to get some cups of coffee and chocolate wafer biscuits, and on the way back I met two monks. They were wearing very thick, black dresses and had beads. They were huge blokes and polite, and even though I expected them to be silent or if not silent then just talking about God, they were talking about fishing. But then I suppose Jesus was a fisherman so maybe they were actually talking about him, and the fishing thing was a distraction. Whatever, they looked at the chocolate wafer biscuits balanced across the lids of my two cups of coffee and said "Looks like you've got everything you need," though I suspect they didn't actually mean that, because I think they knew I didn't have Jesus in my life.

Claire and I sat and drank our coffee and ate our biscuits and the unfinished business carried on hanging over us, and the unspoken words sat in our mouths like prisoners. And the closer we got to Kirkwall the more I knew we would have to face the inevitable, and I knew she knew it too. And I knew that if we had a drink that inevitable would become inescapable, and we would either fade like colour dropped in water or explode. And what was new for me was that I was caught between knowing what I wanted and not knowing at all. For I looked at Claire and knew that the chances of us ever going out were nil, and then I looked at her and all I wanted was to spend every hour with her. And then my phone would ping and Magda would be sending me another text with a picture of her fabulous tits, and I knew my place.

THE DOUGHNUTS THAT MAKE YOU FAINT

When we got back to Stromness, she said "Dinner's on me."

"Yeah?"

"Absolutely. It's the least I can do."

"Great."

I stopped outside The Ferry. She said "I'm going to freshen up. Meet you here at eight?"

"You got it."

Before she got out of the van she leaned towards me and kissed me on the cheek. She was holding Hermann's sculpture. It could have done a lot of damage. "Careful with that," I said.

"Oh yes," she said, "I will be."

I drove back to Shore View, opened a bottle of beer, sat on the pier and called home. Mum answered "Oh, Ed," she said, "I'm glad you called."

"What's up?"

"You know that carbonara you do?"

"Yeah."

"What sort of bacon do you use?"

"It's not bacon, Mum. Don't use bacon."

"I thought not. Then what?"

"Guanciale, Mum. Pork cheeks. Go to Luca's in the Borough. You can get it there. Tell him I sent you."

"And you put the eggs and cheese in last?"

"Yeah. After the spag's cool. Don't let the eggs scramble.

That's the big thing. That and the guanciale."

"Okay."

"Look. I'll send you the recipe."

"Thanks, love," she said, and then I heard Dad shout "Is that Ed?" and she said "Yes," and he said "Pass him over".

"Ed!"

"Dad!"

"How's it going?"

"Good."

"How much longer?"

"A couple of days, tops. I'm going to finish up by the weekend, Monday at the latest, so should be back Wednesday."

"Fair enough."

"You okay?"

"Yeah," he said, "Mum and I are going to Margate tomorrow."

"Sweet."

"We've got a B&B, sea view, tickets to Dreamland, the works..." and he spent the next ten minutes banging on about the old roller-coaster and how back in the day there used to be a doughnut stall that sold doughnuts that would make you faint, they were that good.

"Dad?" I said.

"Yeah?"

"Don't buy Mum any cockles."

"Would I?"

"Dad?"

"What?"

"I've got to go."

"Sure."

"Have a great time."

"Oh we will. You know they've got the biggest dodgem track in the country?"

"Dad?"

"Well, one of the biggest…"

QUELQUES FLEURS SUR LE COU DE MARIE ANTOINETTE

We met in the hotel bar. She'd changed and she'd had a shower but she hadn't washed her hair. That didn't matter. She was wearing her perfume. She said "I had a thought."

"What was it?"

"Fancy fish and chips?"

"Yeah, I think I do."

"Is that cheap-skate?"

"Not if you buy some beers."

"You're on," she said, so we picked up a few cans of something cold from a corner shop, two haddock and chips from a rammed chippy, and found a bench by the harbour.

It was a beautiful evening. There was still warmth in the air and as the sun sank the water shimmered, and a very bright star and/or planet glittered in its place. Fishermen were washing their decks, and a couple of sailing boats were on the water. They were very colourful and going very slowly.

Claire said "Daddy always said he was going to get a little rowing boat, but he never did."

"I'm not sure about rowing boats," I said, and I told her the story of my Dad and me and the dingy on the boating lake in Ramsgate. She thought it was the funniest story she'd ever heard. I told her that it wasn't very funny at the time, and even though the lake wasn't very deep we could have both drowned.

"I almost drowned in Thailand," she said, and she told me she'd gone there on holiday and was staying on a island with palm trees and hammocks and little huts to sleep in, and one morning she got up to go for a swim. "I'm an okay swimmer, at least I thought I was, and I'd swum out about a hundred metres. I turned over and floated for a few minutes, you know, staring up at the sky, looking at the clouds. They were very high. I remember thinking I couldn't believe I was there. I'd always wanted to go to Thailand. Something about a picture book I had when I was a kid. Anyway, when I turned over I could see I'd drifted. There was this rocky headland to the left that was closer than it had been, so I started to swim. But I'd only been going a couple of minutes when I realised I was going nowhere. Then I realised I was going backwards."

"No way…"

"I could feel I was being pulled sideways, and down…"

"Down?"

"Exactly."

"Is that what they call a rip?"

"Yes. And it was weird. They say you should never panic, and I'm pretty cool usually, but I panicked like hell. I was yelling and shouting and waving my arms, but there was no one on the beach, and then I thought okay, now you are drowning, and there was a moment when I felt myself go sort of light inside, as if I was made of foam. And then I thought that if I was made of foam I could float, and that made me feel okay, except then I was closer to the headland, and I could see open water beyond it, and waves. And not just little waves, these were big bastards. So I start yelling waving again, and I'm closer to the rocks and then, out of nowhere, the post boat comes round the headland."

"The post boat?"

"It was one of those long boats you get out there, and it came every morning with the post and stuff for the bar on the beach. It was the only way you could get to the place I was staying. Anyway, it comes round the corner, and this little guy at the front just reaches into the water and pulls me out like I'm a fish, and shakes me and drops me into the bottom of the boat, and the boat hardly slows down at all. And we're bouncing along, and I'm coughing and spluttering and trying to thank this guy who's saved my life, actually saved my life, but he shrugs and laughs. He doesn't speak English, I don't speak any Thai, and when we get to the beach he helps me out of the boat and I hug him and his mate who's been doing the steering thinks that's the funniest thing he's ever seen. The funniest thing. And I almost died..." she said, and she peeled a piece of batter off her fish, popped it in her mouth and chewed.

"That's a hell of a story."

"It was a hell of a morning. And this is a hell of a lot of chips."

"Want me to finish them?"

"Help yourself."

"Sure?"

"Fill your boots."

I tried to think of a story I could tell, but as I'd done the one about the screwdriver in the back of my hand and I didn't think she'd want to hear the one about the time I had to take Barney to the vet because he'd tried to shag a motorbike, I said "Can I ask you something?"

"Anything, Ed."

"That perfume you wear. What is it?"

"Why? You like it?"

"It's amazing."

"Okay. This one is Quelques Fleurs. Bergamot and rose, jasmine, sandalwood and musk." She put her wrist to her nose and then put it to mine. "With a top note of haddock."

What could I say? What could I write? Her wrist touched my nose, my head filled with that smell, I mumbled about nothing.

"It's the perfume that caught Marie Antoinette."

"Who?"

"The Queen of France."

"I didn't think they had a Queen."

"They don't, but they did."

"Okay. And how did a perfume catch her?"

"When the French Revolution kicked off, she tried to get away by disguising herself as a normal person, but she couldn't resist giving herself a few drops of Quelques Fleurs, and even though she almost got away with it, the guys that caught her said that they knew it was her because only a Queen could smell that good."

"So much to learn…" I said.

"What do you mean?"

"What I mean is… I didn't concentrate at school."

"Maybe you didn't," she said, "but that doesn't mean you don't know stuff, does it?"

"I don't know. Maybe. Maybe not."

"I think you know loads."

"Thanks."

"My pleasure."

"No," I said, "mine," and then I leaned towards her and kissed her lips and she didn't flinch, and she put her hand on my back and pulled me towards her so I could feel her heart in its beating, and when we came up for air her face stayed next to mine and she said "Hello, Ed," and I said "Claire…" like her name was a breath against glass.

WARM PASTRY

After the fish was finished and the cans drunk, and the street lights had switched on, we took a stroll down the street. We went past an old building full of paintings and carved stuff called the Pier Arts Centre, and Claire said she'd show me round it in the morning. I said "You know I'm supposed to be working…" and she said "How much more is there to do?"

"Most of the downstairs."

"And how long is that going to take?"

"A couple of days."

" I reckon you can take a couple of hours out of your busy schedule..."

"You're the boss."

"Then you'll chew some art with me tomorrow."

"Okay," I said, and we walked on, and I couldn't think of anything else to say, and the unfinished business put its head around the corner and tapped the side of its head. We passed a pub. Some blokes were outside, smoking. They were busting to say something to Claire but I gave them a stare and they mumbled at the pavement. And then we were alone and the only sounds were the cries of some gulls and our footsteps in the street.

We knew where we were going. We couldn't avoid it. It was like when you're a kid and you're on a bike going downhill and there's a point where the front wheel wobbles and you know the only way you're going to stop is when you ride into a wall. And when you ride into that wall it doesn't hurt half as much as you expect, and all you need to do is get up, brush your knees, straighten your forks and get back on.

She held my hand. It was like holding a warm pastry. She did that thing where she held my arm with her other hand and leant into me and rubbed my arm. We kept good step. She said "Do you gym?"

"No."

"You keep fit."

"That's building. You?"

"Gym?"

"Sometimes. I swim."

"When you're not drowning."

"When I'm not drowning."

When we reached Shore View I said "Fancy a drink?"

"Go on then."

Derek was standing in the alley. He was holding a watering can and looking at some plants in flower pots. When he saw us he did that thing people do when they've been caught but want everyone to think they're innocent. A shifty look, a drop of the head and a mumbled "Evening…"

"And good evening to you, Derek," said Claire. "How are you?"

"Well, you know," he said. "None of us are getting any younger."

"True. But some of us are so much wiser."

"Really?"

"I like to think so."

Derek looked at me and then back at Claire.

"You've met Ed?"

"I have."

"Hello again," I said.

He nodded but didn't say anything to me.

"And how's the book going?" said Claire.

"Slowly," said Derek, "slowly but surely."

His front door opened and Jean poked her head out. "Oh, hello," she said when she saw Claire. "I didn't know you were up."

"Jean. Hi." She stepped forward and they shared an awkward kiss. "Just for a few days."

"Good for you," she said, and she looked at Derek. He said "I'll be in in a minute."

"Your programme's starting," she said.

"I know."

Jean took a step back. "Well, it was nice to see you again."

"And you," said Claire.

Derek put the watering can down. Jean nodded at me and disappeared. Derek said "Well, good evening."

"And a very good evening to you," said Claire.

"Laters," I said.

He didn't snarl but it was close. He just turned and followed his wife, and closed the door, and Claire went for her door, and we stepped into the kitchen.

"Talk about awkward," I said.

"He is just about the weirdest guy I know. God only knows how Jean puts up with him."

"And what's this book he's writing?"

"I think it's something to do with packaging."

"Packaging?"

"A history of packaging."

"That makes sense," I said, and I went to the fridge, took out a bottle of wine and poured a couple of glasses.

"Living room?"

"You want me to light a fire?"

"I think you should," she said, so I did.

RIDING INTO THE WALL

I was in Stromness, which is a town in Orkney.

It was Thursday evening and I was 29 years old.

I was a builder.

I was a better cook than a builder but I was a builder because I could be.

The night before I took a trip to Eday with Claire I tried to count the women I'd slept with, but lost count after thirty. So I did it a different way. I numbered the different ways women had had me, and that was a simple way to do it. So I numbered them and thought about: 1. Easily Distracted, which was easy. When Stu and Mo and I were in Ibiza, I got off with a girl from Bristol. She had a boyfriend at home but said he didn't care and anyway she said, he was giving one to her sister. We'd been drinking and I didn't have to ask twice and we went back to where she was staying, which was a better place than ours. It was on the top floor of a hotel and had a great view from the balcony. You could see the whole of the bay and a hundred yachts but we didn't stop to look at the view because we were at it before the door was closed. So we were at it and after the usual starters we were half way through the main and she was on her knees and I was giving it some serious effort, leaning back and going like a train and then I leaned forward and held her right around the waist and looked over her shoulder and she was on her phone. And I said "What are you doing?" and she said "Texting my mate…" and I said "What are you texting?" and she said "I wanted to see if she was up for a drink later. Want to come?"

And then I thought: 2. Keen As Anything You Want To Mention which was also easy, and that was half the nurses I knew, and I think that's like I said before, because they see so much pain and grief and death all the time so they think forget it, I'm going for it. And half of them did, like their shift started at six and they didn't get off till half seven if they were lucky and all they'd had was a yoghurt, an apple and a cheese sandwich. Most of the time they didn't think about it, they just enjoyed it, they loved it, they necked a bottle of wine and loved it again unlike 3. Some Very Concerned Students who were worried about the world and how it was being destroyed and everything. I suppose they thought they should be experiencing more from what they were doing than what they were getting, but they were so worried about Brexit and meat and plastic that they forgot that what you get is what you do, and they just lay there with a look like they were thinking about how to solve the problem of homelessness. And when I looked into some of their eyes I could see them in thirty years time as they found the thing that was so plain when they were young. And then I was with 4. Intense Hippies who were the funniest women I ever slept with, though everyone says the last thing you need to do is laugh when you're at it. The half dozen Intense Hippies I went out with went at it like they were waiting for something, so all the time I'm at it it's like they're somewhere else, not necessarily in another country, but probably on another planet which is, when I think about it, not funny at all. And a couple of the Intense Hippies I slept with did this thing where they stopped suddenly and asked me to laugh and be mindful, and I had no idea what mindful was or what I was meant to do with it even if I knew what it was, and then I went soft and couldn't carry on because I was confused. Hippies. They're a nightmare.

You haven't gone truly loco until you've been with 5. who has

Watched Too Much Porn and doesn't care who knows it, and one of these worked on reception at a top hotel in Knightsbridge, and that bloke from that movie had checked in last week, and just talking to his PA made her wet, and she was wondering why she was like that girl in that movie with Hugh Grant when he's the Prime Minister and she's living in a terrace and her Dad calls her fat or something, which is unfair because she's not. And she was wild but because she had to get up at some ungodly hour I knew it was lost before we began, which was a shame because one of her nipples was inverted, and I liked popping it out of its shell.

6. was one of the most distracting women I ever went with, and she was a Hummer as she hummed all the way through, and don't think it was something tuneful like stuff out of Les Miserables, this was just random snatches of stuff that made no sense at all. The week before I'd been with one of the hippies of my life and I remember thinking "Am I doing something wrong?" and maybe I was. Maybe I was being selfish or not being attentive or something, but I can't say for certain, though I should say that 7. A Religious Night could be a tad odd. Magda was a first-class religious night in a Roman Catholic style, and used to mutter something in Polish when we'd finished and she thought I was asleep, and I know she was muttering to her God because I'd hear the word "Jesus". Even though she'd sort of given up her religion I think she felt guilty and was hoping Jesus would forgive her or something, but I don't know for sure. I never asked her.

8. would be Make Up Love, and there were a few of those. I usually met them when I was up West on a weekend, though sometimes they'd come to one of the clubs in the arches under the Bridge. They looked so up for it and would show some top moves, and give you a look that said you'd scored. But once you were alone they changed and it wasn't about busting the moves any

more, just the thought that you might ruin their make up. And that made me think that they weren't dressed and dancing for the lads, they were dressed and dancing for their girlfriends, and that turned out to be true and confused me. But it didn't confuse me as much as 9. which was a Quickie In The Van, which never did it for me, especially when they wiped themselves afterwards and dropped the tissues on the floor for Dad to find in the morning. That was gross, and I'm not a fan of gross.

I wrote all this not because I wanted to brag but because I wanted to understand my past and how I got to where I was in Stromness on the Thursday evening with Claire, who was beyond writing about. I did think that I would try and write about what happened after I lit the fire in her father's old house, but it would be difficult. So here's the thing.

THE BEST DINNER I EVER
HAD WITHOUT A BAR

I won't name the restaurant but it's on a street in north London. It's a small place and the window frames are painted dark blue. The chairs are bentwood, the tables are covered in checked cloths and the cutlery is nothing special. You could walk by without noticing the menu, which is posted in a glass box by the door, which sticks. It's not the sort of place where celebrities go, though there was a picture of Nick Cave on the wall when I was there. He was tall and dawdling. I don't think Nick Cave ever ate in the restaurant I won't name but the owner liked the man's music. I like Nick Cave's music too, but not when I'm driving.

I ate alone. I know. Restaurants don't like people who eat alone. They think someone who eats alone is unhappy, and they don't want unhappiness infecting other people in the restaurant but I knew Sylvie, the chef. I'd done some decorating for her, and she wasn't worried about what I might look like to the other people who were eating there. All she worried about was whether I enjoyed my dinner.

Things got off to a flier. The place was quiet and I was given a good table. It was in a corner by the window, which is the top spot for me. I like having my back to a wall and I like to look at stuff between courses, which were matched with wine. Or maybe the courses were being introduced to the wine with the thought that something might develop later. Who knew? Maybe Sylvie. Her restaurant is on a side street that leads off a busy road in the centre of the city. Interesting people walked by, and dogs.

The meal started with an amuse-bouche, which I'd say is the cottage cheese of loving, and cottage cheese isn't cheese. But the waiter said Sylvie had made this amuse-bouche just for me. Enough potato and Roquefort soup to fill a shot glass, and a wafer-thin slice of toasted rye bread cut like a little scar, so I gave it a go. The soup was smooth and creamy and strong, and the bread crunched like the moon on a cold night, or a bold tinker. It came with a small glass of Burgundy – the waiter told me to expect some bitterness in the wine, which is just as well because I wouldn't have known.

Things got serious with the starter which was fishcake but this wasn't just any old knocked-up fishcake fried in a pan and dumped on a side plate with some foam and a spotting of something pale. This was made from mackerel and smoked eel and topped with a poached egg that wobbled like a troubled chin. There were three mussels on the plate too, and a patch of samphire in white butter. Every bite was like being on the front at Margate in a storm, or Ramsgate. The waiter had offered Chablis with this plate, and once he'd done his job he kept his distance. He was watching me but he didn't move. He didn't interrupt me to ask how things were. He was quiet. And when some other people came into the restaurant he offered them a table on the far side of the room, and went back to his station.

For the main course I went with a fillet steak cut from an animal that used to live on a farm outside Teignmouth, which is a seaside town in Devon. The meat had been rubbed with goose fat before being cooked for three minutes, rested for two and served with roasted shallots, a confit of charlotte potatoes and a morel and wine sauce. Before it arrived, the waiter poured me a glass of Pinot Noir, told me to swill it around and give it a good sniff. I did as I was told, and had a mouthful. Then the plate was bought to my table.

The shallots popped and melted, the potatoes were potatoes but nothing like any potatoes I'd eaten, and the sauce tasted earthy and sweet and like dates. And the steak was a pillow that didn't need the knife. A spoon would have done it. The goose fat lifted the meat so it seem to float an inch from the plate. When I took the first bite I thought this must last. It had to. I rolled it around my mouth. I swallowed. I drank some wine. The waiter told me the wine was chewy. I didn't agree with that.

I ate slowly. I tried every combination. Steak on its own, steak with some sauce, sauce with a shallot, a shallot with a sliver of steak, sauce on its own, potato on its own, potato with shallot, shallot with potato and some sauce – each was perfect. A piece of steak in my mouth, and before I swallowed, a sip of wine. Better. And when I'd finished, I closed my eyes and sat back and let the tastes come back to me, and the waiter didn't need to say anything.

I thought about pudding. I thought about pudding for ten minutes and then I went for it. I chose a warm Jamaican ginger cake with a coconut sorbet and a knife of spiced pineapple on the side. This arrived with a small glass of the thickest wine I've ever drunk. Muscat. It stuck to the inside of my mouth. I wasn't sure when I was drinking it but I knew all about it afterwards.

Cheese? I had cheese. I had a wedge of Bucheron and a knob of Bleu des Causses. and a glass of a strong wine called Maury. This was sweet and red and better than the cheese though the cheese was fabulous, and then I closed my eyes and sat back again. Some more people had come to the restaurant. They were sitting close to me but I didn't care. They were talking to each other. They talked about something that had happened at their work and they laughed and then they talked some more except this time it was about food. The waiter asked me if I wanted coffee. I did want coffee. I had an espresso. I drank the espresso. Sylvie came from the kitchen. She was busy now but wanted to say hello. I thanked her. She asked me if I could drop by some time next week to look at her pantry. It needed tiling. I said I'd tile anything she wanted, and she laughed.

I tell the story of the best dinner I ever had because I couldn't tell the story of the first night I spent with Claire, but everything about that first night matched the best dinner I ever had, and will always be as the bird that finds its cup. The bird flies, the bird looks and the bird sees, and as the bird lands she folds her wings slowly and tucks them in, and leans her head to one side. And if it's raining she shields the place she's found from the damp, and keeps it warm and dry with her pretty chest.

THE ECHO OF A DEAD
WOMAN'S WHISTLING

I opened my eyes. It was early. It was about half six. The sky was pink. My mouth was fine. I put my hand over my face. I was there. I looked at the ceiling and I looked at Claire. She was sleeping. She was lying face down on the bed. I pulled the duvet back a few inches. I put my hand on her back. For a moment I imagined I wasn't a builder and my hands were soft. She turned towards me and opened her eyes. They opened slowly. When she saw me she wasn't surprised. She wasn't shocked. I was shocked. Scent came off her like a drift of plaster dust on one of those summer after-noons when you shouldn't be working but have to. She smiled at me and whispered "Good morning".

I whispered "Hello." I stared at her. I reached out, touched the scar on her chin and said "Tea?"

"In a minute."

I said "Can I kiss it?"

"What?"

"Your scar."

She said "Of course."

I kissed it. She tasted of salt and made the sound a cracked egg makes when it slides into the bowl. I said "How did you get it?"

She said "I slipped on a Lego brick and hit myself on the corner of a box."

I said "What sort of box?"

"It was the box Daddy kept his microscope in. Old school."

"How old were you?"

She sniffed and said "Six."

I said "I've got scars."

"I know."

"Want to see them?"

"I have."

She had.

"Can I tell you a story?"

She said "I'm not sure I believe your stories."

"There's nothing wrong with my stories."

"I never said there was." She sniffed again. "What's that smell?"

"Paint?"

"No. almonds. Marzipan. I can smell marzipan."

"It's paint."

"Really?"

"Yeah," I said, and "Cup of tea?"

"That sounds like a plan."

I went downstairs. While I was waiting for the kettle to boil I stood in the living room and looked out of the window. The harbour and its water were a dream. I made the tea. I went back to the living room. I looked at the harbour and the water again. The sky was orange now. I poured the tea and took the mugs back to bed. She sat up, sipped and lay down again. I said "I don't know what to say."

"You don't have to say anything."

I said nothing.

The obvious is easy.

I'm not going to explain and I'm not going to tell, but I will say that an hour later, when she came back from the shower she dressed in front of me, and my heart was full of her. She said "I'm going back to The Ferry. I need fresh pants."

"Want to borrow some of mine?"

"Yeah, that'd work," she said.

"I'll get on with some work."

"Okay. "

THE ORCADIAN WAS FIRST PUBLISHED IN 1854

I worked hard. I'd done half the living room by eleven. Or was it most of the living room? I don't remember. Did I care? I didn't. I wasn't normal anymore. I stopped for coffee. I was pushing the plunger into the pot when Claire came back. She was wearing one of those striped shirts French people with baguettes wear but she didn't have a baguette. She had the local newspaper. It was called The Orcadian. I poured two mugs of the coffee and we went outside and sat on the pier and watched the boats, and a load of ducks spent a load of time making wheezy noises at the bottom of the steps. It was like they were having a conversation.

"What are they?" I said. There were black and white ones and brown ones, and a crowd of smaller ones.

She got up, looked at them, sat down again and said "Eider ducks. They gossip."

"I hear them in the night."

"The mums are the brown ones. They organise crèches for their babies. They're the cleverest ducks out there."

"Eider ducks. Okay. I'm going to have to make a list."

"Good idea." She sipped her coffee. "And good coffee."

"Thanks."

"You still up for chewing some art?"

"I think so."

"After lunch?"

"Sounds like a plan."

She put her hand on my thigh. I put my hand on her hand. It was as natural as indicating and moving into the middle lane. She said "Mind if I hang around?"

"It's your place. You do what you want."

"I don't want to get in the way."

"You won't."

"I'll read the paper."

"Sure."

She leaned towards me. She kissed me on the lips. Her face was like a menu.

"Great."

I went inside and carried on.

It was easy work. I was using a roller.

I'd been working for twenty minutes when I heard her shout "What the hell!"

I saw her through the window.

She got up.

She was holding the paper. She came and found me. She pointed at a headline in the paper. "Ed?"

"Yes."

"You know anything about this?"

The headline was about the stolen bowl. It read "VALUABLE BOWL STOLEN IN STROMNESS". There was the picture Marcus had given plod, and a couple of paragraphs describing the bowl and how Lucie Rie was one of the most important potters ever.

"I do," I said.

"And?"

"And... and I thought Marcus would have told you."

"Marcus?"

"Yes."

"Marcus is…" She took a deep breath.

I said "I was going to tell you about it but…"

"Stop," she said. She held up her hand like plod would stop the traffic. "Please. Just stop talking…" and she went upstairs. I heard her in the bedroom. She did some crashing around. A couple of minutes later she came downstairs again. She was carrying a biscuit tin. She put it on the table and took off the lid. The bowl was inside, sitting in a nest of bubble wrap and newspaper. "I put it in with Mum's stuff when Marcus and I were up for the funeral. It's my fault. I never thought to tell him."

"Ah…" I said. "Okay. Okay…"

"So…"

"Yeah…"

She tapped the newspaper. "How did this happen?"

"When Marcus was here he packed up a load of your Dad's things, but couldn't find it. I said that maybe you'd taken it, but he said you wouldn't do that. So he decided it had been stolen. Called the police, and… and there it is."

She laughed. "Why didn't he call me?"

"I don't know."

She rummaged in her bag, pulled out her phone and dialled a number. "I hid it because I didn't want it stolen, and now… Marcus? Hi. Yeah…" She stood up and went outside, and for the next ten minutes she walked up and down outside the house, talking and waving her arms. When she came back inside she tossed the phone on the table, said "Sometimes I wonder, how did my brother get where he is. He can be such a twat. But I suppose his sister is too…"

"We'd better call the police."

"That might be an idea. Know the number?"

"It's in there." I pointed to the plastic box thing next to the old fashioned phone.

"I'll give them a call."

"Okay."

She looked for the number and said "Marcus told me to tell you he's sorry for the trouble. He said he didn't think you got on with the local copper."

"You could say that."

"He did."

"He was just a copper."

She dialled the number. The call went through to an answer machine. She left a message, hung up and said "An apology from Marcus is something. I've never had one…"

"So can I see what the fuss was all about?"

"What do you mean?"

I pointed at the biscuit tin.

"Oh, of course." She peeled the bubble wrap away, lifted the bowl out and put it in the middle of the table.

"You know who Lucie Rie was?"

"Marcus told me about her, but I've never seen any of her stuff. But I get it…"

"What do you mean?"

"It's beautiful."

It wasn't as big as I'd thought it would be – maybe twelve centimetres across the top and seven high. It was shaped like the sort of hat you might see a Chinese person wearing in an old film, and the raised bit it sat on was the size of a marshmallow. But what made it was the colour, which was green, but not just any sort of green. This green was pale in some places and darker in others, as if it was actually moving over the surface of the bowl. The lip was golden and speckled. There were places where the green looked almost blue, but I think that was a trick of the light.

I said "Can I pick it up?"

"Carefully, Ed…"

I picked it up. It was too light. I put it down again.

Claire said "Listen" and she flicked its rim with her finger nail. It rang a note and the note hung in the air over the table. "And again…" and she flicked it again.

"I don't know what to say."

"I always used to think it was the sound of Lucie Rie whistling in her workshop."

"Yeah," I said. "I think it is."

She flicked it again, said "Hello Lucie," and to me "I think I owe you lunch."

"What are you cooking?"

"Buying," she said.

ART IS THE FUTURE OF THE WORLD

We ate at The Ferry. I had the seafood chowder and asked for enough bread to fill my pockets. Claire had a ploughman's lunch with extra cheese. I said "I had a ploughman's lunch last week."

She said "Did you?"

"Yes," I said. "He was furious."

"Stop it," she said.

"Sorry."

"No you're not."

"I am."

"Is that a fisherman's pie?"

"No."

We were made for each other.

The chowder was delicious.

I added extra pepper.

The bread was big.

I was in shock.

I wasn't sure if I was in shock because Lucie Rie's bowl was no longer stolen or because I was in love. It was hard to say because I had never been in love before, so I ate my chowder. It was delicious. I had more pepper than I needed. I said "What a day."

"What a night. What a day."

"And it's only half one."

She looked at her watch. "It's a quarter to two."

After lunch we went to the Pier Arts Centre, which is a converted shed full of art. There were pictures and sculptures. It wasn't as big as Tate Modern but some of the stuff was just as weird.

You went in through a glass door and there was a shop where you could buy expensive pencils. A woman was sat behind a desk. She had a big smile and was pale. She was wearing a coat. I think she was cold because I was cold in there and I don't feel the cold.

Claire led the way. We went upstairs. The rooms were white and bright. The architect and builder had done a good job of the place. There was plenty of glass and light, and you could stand at one end of a room and see the edges of paintings against angles and sculptures through openings in the walls. Claire said it was "severe" but I didn't know about that. I think they'd used some quality paint and the finish was good though I spotted some blemishes, mainly in the jointing.

They had a few pictures by Alfred Wallis, who was the bloke who did the painting my old man's mate had inherited, the one that went for fifty eight grand. You could get close to them and see how the bloke had put the paint on, and see the edges of the cardboard he painted on. The more I looked at the pictures the more I could see that they were really good and not something a kid could do at playgroup, not unless you had a very clever kid. The boats and people were sort of stretched and flat. And there were some sculptures by a woman called Barbara Hepworth, and some of these were on the window sills so if you looked at them from the right direction them seemed to be floating on the harbour. One of the best of her things was a big wooden ball that had been carved out in a way that didn't seem to begin or end anywhere, and then she'd painted this carved bit with white paint. I said "That's okay. I want it."

"You can't have it," said Claire.

Some other visitors in the gallery looked at us.

"Is there any of Hermann's stuff here?"

"He had an exhibition last year, but I don't think there's any-thing on show. You might be able to get a book in the shop."

I think my favourite thing was another sculpture by Barbara Hepworth of two heads close together. One of the heads was a woman's and the others was a kid's, but you couldn't tell for sure. If you saw the thing from a distance you'd probably think it was a blob of snot, but when you got up close it was obvious that this was a mum with a flat top kissing her baby's forehead. The heads were made from alabaster, which is the rock plaster is made from. Barbara Hepworth had scratched one of the woman's eyes on but hadn't done it very well, and she'd cocked up the kid's eye too, but I think it was these mistakes that made the rest of the thing so good.

We spent an hour in the Pier Arts Centre, and although I had a good look in the shop I couldn't find a book about Hermann. I did buy a postcard of a bloke in a boat by Alfred Wallis. I was going to send it to Dad. We stepped out into the street and stood there for a moment. A gang of cruise ship passengers were coming towards us. Claire and I had a quiet moment and then I said "I have to get back to work," and she said "And I suppose I have to pack."

"Pack?"

"Afraid so. I have to go home tomorrow."

"Okay."

"Work on Monday. Back to reality." She took my hand. "Have I told you about my work?"

"A bit."

"It's rubbish," she said.

"You said."

"I'm sorry."

I shook my head and said "Never say sorry to me."

"Why not?"

"Just because."

"Because what?"

I knew what I wanted to say but I couldn't, so we walked on. We walked on for a couple of minutes and then I said "And the dream is over."

"I don't know," she said.

"You don't know what?"

"It depends."

"On what?"

"On what the dream is."

NETS ARE NOT FOR THE DUTCH

We both knew what the dream was. She was kidding me and I wasn't kidding her. Stories don't have endings, they're just abandoned. They're left like a dog no one wants, tied to a lamp post on a strange street. I went back to paint a wall and she went to pack her bag and look forward to saying goodbye to Stromness and getting back to her flat and her top of the range kitchen appliances that don't get the use they should do. I hadn't even seen the inside of her hotel room. I wanted to see where she'd slept her other nights, and I wanted to see if she kept it tidy. I like tidy.

When I reached Shore View I stopped for a moment and then carried on walking until I reached Elise and Alec's house. I looked up at the plastic owl on the roof. It looked back at me. I could see Elise. She was in the kitchen. I remembered something someone had told me when I was in Amsterdam. I was in a bar, and a woman told me that Dutch people don't like curtains. They don't like curtains because it proves they've got nothing to hide. Either that or they want people to admire their knick-knacks. Elsie had a few knick-knacks on her kitchen window sill. One of them was a blue and white windmill. I walked up the garden path and knocked on the front door. She answered it. She was wearing an apron and her hands and arms were covered in flour. The delicious smells of baking were in the house and I said "Oh hi. I was wondering if Alec is in?"

"In the workshop, young man, in the workshop." She clapped her hands. A little cloud of flour blew up in front of her. "Forgive me. I have a cake to finish."

"Of course."

"In the workshop."

"Thanks."

She wasn't wrong. Alec was sitting at his work bench. He was in the middle of attaching cotton to a row of half-built masts. He was wearing very thick special glasses. When he saw me he put down a tiny pair of tweezers and said "Thank God! An excuse to stop…"

"I'm sorry," I said. "I didn't mean to…"

"You, young man, say nothing but sorry."

"I know," I said, "but I thought you should be the first to hear."

"Hear what?"

"Well…"

"Well?"

"We found the bowl. Lucie Rie's bowl…"

He took off his glasses and said "But this is excellent! Well done you! Where was it?"

"In a biscuit tin."

"In a biscuit tin… superb. And how did it end up in a biscuit tin?"

"It was all a bit stupid…" I said, and when I'd finished the story he looked at his watch and said "I think this calls for a drink."

"I don't know. I should be working."

"Nonsense. You can have one of Elise's specials."

So I followed Alec back to the house and we sat in the kitchen and drank glasses of something called Tesseltje, which was a liqueur from an island called Texel in the north of the Netherlands. It was where Elise had been born, and she told me that parts of Orkney reminded her of her island. "Except the sheep," she said.

"The sheep in Orkney are prettier than Texel sheep."

"The houses are prettier there," said Alec.

"Some of them."

"And the weather's better."

"Sometimes. It depends. In the winter it's just as bad."

"True."

"It can be worse."

The drink was red and sweet and made from a secret recipe, but I tasted cinnamon and cloves, and something else. Almonds, I think. It wasn't strong but it was strong enough, so by the time I got back to Shore View I was feeling snoozy, and thought I'd sit down with a cup of coffee before getting back to it, and then I decided not to have the coffee and just get on with the sit down, and five minutes later I was asleep.

MOST OF THE THINGS DIDN'T HAPPEN BECAUSE IT WAS A NOVEL

Claire woke me with a kiss on my mouth. "Ah," she said, and she took me round the waist and pinched.

"Ow!"

"The worker…"

"Yes. I er…" I sat up.

"I bet you did." She was smiling. She had very white teeth. I think she had a good dentist. I think she had a hygienist too. I did some work at a dental surgery once, so I know about dentists and hygienists. Of all the workers in the world, dentists are the most likely to commit suicide, but that's not because they have to look in people's manky mouths every day, it's because their cupboards are full of powerful drugs. But I didn't say anything about that, I just said "I…"

"You?"

"I went to see Elsie and Alec, your Dad's friends."

"I know who Elsie and Alec are."

"I wanted to tell them the bowl wasn't nicked…"

"Of course you did." She sniffed. "And did you have something to drink there?"

"Yeah. Why?"

"I can smell it. Almonds?"

"Yeah. Almonds. It was this vile Dutch stuff. It was a bit like mouthwash. Thick mouthwash. Then I got back here and the next thing I knew…"

"Is you're having an afternoon nap."

"Yeah."

"That's a slippery slope, Ed."

"I know. My dad has one. Sometimes standing up."

"I want to meet your dad."

"That sounds serious."

"I don't want to marry him…"

"He's already married."

"There you go then. Tea?"

"Ta."

So Claire made the tea and I got busy in the kitchen with a roller. She sat in the living room and read a book. It was about Russia. Okay, it wasn't about Russia. It was set in Russia. It was about people, and it was a novel, so most of the things that happened didn't happen. And the person that wrote the novel used a voice but it wasn't his voice. It was the voice of the person who was writing the novel, but he wasn't the novelist. I worked for an hour. Maybe an hour and a half. I don't know. It was one of those days. My brain was hopping all over the place, and I couldn't stop it.

A BOOKLET COMES WITH THE BOTTLE

On the last evening with Claire I cooked dinner. I made a mushroom risotto and a green salad. There were some cherry tomatoes on the side but we didn't eat them.

We sat in the kitchen. She'd bought a bottle of wine. It tasted of pears. She said "I always think a plate of risotto isn't going to be enough, but it's always too much."

"Salad?"

"Thanks."

"Tomatoes?"

"No thanks."

There were too many things I wanted to say and things I wanted to ask, but I didn't know where to start. She knew it too, so for an hour or so we skated around the edges. We weren't being cowards but we were afraid. She said something about how her flat would feel odd after Stromness, and I apologised for not having any parmesan. She said that when she was a kid she used to have a gerbil called Pepper. I told her about Bubbles my rabbit. She asked me where I went to school and when I told her the name of my primary school she said "No way!" and said that she used to live round the corner. "Maybe we saw each other when we were kids!"

"Maybe," I said, "but I wasn't into girls then. Footie, Claire, footie…"

When my phone pinged she didn't ask me who was texting and

when, ten minutes later, hers did the same but with a different tone, I said nothing. I didn't want to be regretful but it was hard not to let the risotto go cold. So when she opened another bottle of wine and we went through to the living room, she said the word that would start the end. She said "Look…"

"Yeah?"

"It has to be said," she said.

"What has?"

"Last night. I know we'd had a few…"

"More than a few," I said. "We were hammered."

"But I meant what I said."

"What did you say?"

"Don't you remember?"

"You said a lot of things. We both did."

"I seem to remember that all you said was 'Oh my God…' You said that a lot."

"Yeah, I know. Sorry about that. I was just amazed."

"Me too, Ed, me too."

"But not in the same way."

"How do you know that?"

"Claire. I'll tell you a secret. Well, it's not really a secret. It's just a thing…"

"Go on then."

"The first time I saw you I just thought, 'Wow...'"

"Wow?"

"I thought you were a knock-out."

"Okay…"

"It's true."

"And your point is?"

"My point is, I thought you were totally out of my league. Were? Are."

"Oh please."

"I'm a builder, Claire."

"And what's that got to do with the price of eggs?"

"Everything. I don't know stuff. That art this afternoon. I was watching you when you looked at it. You know what it's about, you understand it."

"Now you're talking crap, Ed. Pure, unadulterated crap. I don't understand it anymore than you do."

"Okay, bad example."

"Then give me a good one."

"Okay. That book you're reading. That Russian novel."

"It's an overwritten load of self-pitying nonsense. Next."

"I don't know. Stuff you know. That stuff about the perfume you wear. All about the Queen of France…"

"It's in a little booklet that comes with the bottle."

"Okay. Then…"

"What are you trying to tell me?"

"I already said."

"Remind me."

I shook my head. "What's the point?"

"Then let me remind you."

"Go on then."

"Last night I said that I'd never met anyone like you."

"Is that a good thing?"

"It's a very good thing. Very good indeed. I meet a lot of people, Ed."

"Okay…"

"So, seeing as you won't say it, what I'm saying is this. If you want to see me again, just give me a call."

"What? In London?"

"No. In Reykjavík."

"Where's that?"

"In London, Ed. London."

"Oh."

"Oh? Is that all you can say."

"But what about Anthony?"

"I could ask the same about Magda."

"She's dumped me."

"Hasn't stopped her texting."

"She'll get tired of that soon enough. Will Anthony?"

"I'm seeing him next week. He'll get the news then."

"And what news is that?"

"That his Harlequins scarf doesn't need to feel jealous any more."

"Okay…"

"And if he wants to collect his toothbrush from mine, he needn't bother. I'll have chucked it. I need to make some room in my bathroom."

Her voice, her lips, her bathroom. London. When I thought about London and her being there, I felt something move beneath my skin. Something, I suppose, like ice slowly melting and dripping in the voids that had grown inside me. And although I didn't know where she lived in Greenwich, I hoped that she had a view of the river. Or if not the river, then a pond.

CLAIRE'S ROOM AT THE FERRY

The smell of paint was giving Claire a headache so we went back to The Ferry. Her room was on the top floor. It was small and warm, and had a great view. I counted seven boats and fifteen clouds. The ceiling was low and angled. There were toiletries in the bathroom. I had a bottle of wine in a bag and a toothbrush in my pocket. There were glasses so I poured and then I got on the bed because there wasn't a lot of space.

I'd never seen a woman take her clothes off like Claire took her clothes off in her room in The Ferry. She didn't simply take them off or even shed them. She peeled. And I don't think she did what she did because I was watching her. She did it because that's how she always undressed. Every movement was slow and deliberate and without any sort of embarrassment. She didn't try to make herself smaller or bigger, or hold her stomach in, or push her tits out. She didn't brush her naked shoulders or touch her hair. The folds in her skin, the sprinkle of freckles on the back of her neck, the way she walked to the bathroom on tiptoes, the way she came back brushing her teeth and then went back, the curl of her back, the little knobs of her elbows, her nipples and the way her fringe bobbed when she lowered her head and looked at me, and then she slid in next to me like a crowd folds into a bus, and wrapped her arms around my arms, and that smell, that Queen of France scent, and she said "Every time I get close to you I smell marzipan."

"Or almonds?"

"I don't know, Ed. We pay you to do a job and what happens? You go to sleep on the job. It's appalling."

"I'm sorry."

"Are you on checkatrade?"

"Of course. Why?"

She laughed. "You'll never work again. Marcus and I are going to screw you. You're going to be toast."

"Please don't."

"Okay," she said, "kiss me instead."

I did as I was told and more, and then we drank some more wine and talked about how some things that people think are important are not important at all, and I was telling her about this bloke Dad and I did a job for, and how he lived in this massive place in Knightsbridge and had an underground garage with six cars but he was the angriest, unhappiest person I'd ever met, but my story had sent her to sleep.

I watched her sleep.

People sometimes say that people look peaceful when they're sleeping, but Claire didn't. She looked like she was trying to remember where she'd put something, and then she looked worried, and then, after about twenty minutes, she licked her lips and mumbled "I'll do it later…"

I wasn't sure what to do. Should I wake her? Hold her? Do nothing? She answered the question for me. She woke up, looked at me and said "Yes?"

"You were talking…" I said. "You were talking in your sleep."

"I'm sorry. I do that." She reached up and touched my hair. "What did I say?"

"Something about doing something later."

"Procrastination. Another fault."

"I see no fault," I said.

She turned away from me and said "Damn."

"What?"

"No water."

"Here," I said. There was a bottle on my side of the bed. "There you go."

"Cheers," she said, and she sat up and took a swig. I watched her neck do that thing when you swallow, and then she passed the bottle back to me.

"No," I said, "keep it…"

"Thanks," she said, and she lay down again and rested her head on my chest. I know she was listening to the beat of my heart. She tapped me with the tips of my fingers and looked up at me and then closed her eyes and went "Mmm…" and a couple of minutes later she was asleep again, and making the sort of sounds a small animal would make if it found a safe place in a hedge, or a wall.

GOODBYE

In the morning I took Claire to the airport. We looked at local pro-
duce in glass cabinets, and at some mosaic pictures on the walls,
and we drank a cup of coffee. I didn't feel like eating a piece of
cake and nor did she. We didn't say a lot but I stayed with her until
the flight was called. She picked up her bag. She'd packed Lucie
Rie's bowl. I said "Don't get it nicked."

"And no drinking on the job."

"Don't worry. I'm not staying here longer than I have to."

"And why's that?"

"You have to ask?"

"Look…"

"I'm a bit like Hermann."

"How's that?"

"I can't do goodbyes."

"Nor can I."

"So go."

"Okay."

"Really. Go."

"I've gone," she said, and she kissed me and I held her and
then she went and joined the queue for security and then she was
gone and I couldn't see her anymore, so I went back to the van
and drove back to Stromness and got the roller going again in the
kitchen.

DRINKING IN THE PUB

That evening, after I'd finished most of the kitchen and eaten some fish and chips, I went for a pint. I couldn't face The Ferry so I found another pub. It was dark and rammed with locals and divers. The carpet was wrong and there were pictures on the walls of sinking battleships. I found a spot at a corner table. I didn't want to talk to anyone. I checked my phone. Nothing.

I wanted to drink beer and watch people and drink some more beer. The beer was okay. So when I saw Joe and Ellen I tried to ignore them but they didn't want to ignore me. It was only half eight but she was hammered. He had a black eye. She yelled "Oi! London!" and pushed her way through the crowd. He followed her but I don't think he wanted to. I think he wanted to be in another pub, in another town, in another country. I wasn't going to be rude so I nodded but I didn't say anything.

"Yeah London!" she yelled again and now she was standing in front of me. "I found it."

"Hello Ellen," I said. "Joe."

He gave me one of those nods you get when you're sharing knowledge without knowing that you're sharing.

"I found it."

"What did you find?"

"That bowl. So give me the money."

"You found the bowl?"

"Yes."

"Okay. Show me."

"Oh no." She shook her head. "I know your game. Money first,

London. You're not getting me like that."

"Okay. So how much did we say?"

"A grand."

"Just the one? I thought it was two. A bowl like that. It's worth a fortune…"

"Yeah." She leaned towards me. There was dried spit at the corners of her mouth, and her left eye was wandering. "Two grand, London."

"Okay," I said, and I fished in my pocket, pulled out some shrapnel and looked at it. It sat nicely in the palm of my hand. I said "Seeing as we found it yesterday, and it's now on a plane back to London, I suppose twenty pence will have to do…" I tossed a coin onto the table and put the rest back in my pocket. I suppose it wasn't the cleverest thing to do, but I didn't care. At that moment, with a pint and a half down my neck and the job almost done and the feeling that whatever Claire had said about seeing each other again in London was crap because I knew what we'd had was just like some holiday fling like the one I had in Ibiza and another I had in Amsterdam and ones she'd have had in Mauritius or Rome, and at that moment the twenty pence on the table was me laughing because I couldn't laugh myself. But Ellen didn't think it was funny. She looked at the coin and her face went as red as her hair and she took a swing at me. It was a vague right hook but didn't go anywhere, and was easy enough to dodge. She tried to follow up with a little left jab, but before it was out of the blocks Joe was on her back, she'd lost balance and crashed onto the table. It was a poor mess – wood, glass, beer, carpet, this enormous woman flailing and yelling, and Joe caught another shiner on top of the one he already had. I just stepped away and stepped over Ellen and carried on stepping, and the crowd parted like hair, and then I was outside on the orange street of Stromness, in the drizzle.

I stood outside the pub for a moment and listened to the racket and wondered if the plod who turned up would be the same plod who turned up to discuss valuable bowls with Marcus and me, and then I walked back to Shore View and sat in the kitchen and opened a bottle of Corncrake and drank it slowly.

I sat in the kitchen and I looked at my phone. She'd be home by now, unpacking her bag, putting Lucie Rie's bowl on a shelf, pouring herself a glass of wine and wondering what she'd been thinking. I looked at my phone but I didn't get a call and I didn't get a text. I looked at the walls. I drank some more beer and an hour later I was asleep.

IT DIDN'T TAKE ME LONG TO FINISH THE JOB AND TIDY UP

It didn't take me long to finish the job and tidy up. The walls were white, the van was packed with the stuff Marcus and Claire wanted, and at a quarter to five on Monday morning I was driving onto the ferry to Scrabster. The big blue Viking didn't care about me and I didn't care about him, the size of the boat, the rivets or the weight of it. I was too tired.

I went upstairs and sat on a bench on the deck, and when we started to move I stood at the railing and watched Stromness go. I saw the window of Claire's room at The Ferry, and I saw Shore View and the pier where we'd sat, and I saw the owl on the roof of Elsie and Alec's house. I didn't see Joe or Ellen. Then the boat went round the corner and the town disappeared.

I went downstairs and found a seat by a window and I sat and watched Orkney disappear, and when it was gone I closed my eyes. I had a long drive and I didn't want to think about it. I didn't want to think about the drive, the hotel I'd have to sleep in and motorway food, so I didn't. I caught up on the sleep I was owed and an hour and a half later, when I was told to go down to the car deck and occupy my vehicle, I did as I was told.

It was still early. I checked my phone. Nothing. I turned it off. No distractions. I drove. Nothing. I did as I was told, and didn't stop until I reached Inverness. It was eleven o'clock. I filled the tank, grabbed a coffee and a couple of doughnuts and parked up to eat. I checked my phone. Dad had left a message about how he and Mum had decided to spend an extra day in Margate, the builders' merchants we use had texted about a special offer on multi-packs of cement and plaster, and Claire had tried to call me. She hadn't left a message. I finished the first doughnut, swilled my mouth with coffee and called back. Her phone went straight through to voicemail. I said "Oh, hi. It's me. Ed. You tried to call. I'm driving south, so maybe talk later…" There was something else I wanted to say but I couldn't find the right words, so I hung up and ate the second doughnut. I ate and imagined her in her office, in a meeting with half a dozen other suits, picking up her phone and seeing my name and shaking her head and turning it off and apologising. "Sorry," she'd say. "Nothing important. You were saying, Clive?" And Clive would give her one of his winning smiles, check the time and adjust his tie. I was licking the sugar off my fingers and finishing the coffee when she called back.

"Ed?"

"Hey."

"I'm sorry. I was in a meeting."

"No worries. You okay?"

"Yes thanks. Where are you?"

"Parked on a garage forecourt outside Inverness."

"Lovely."

"Two doughnuts and a cup of coffee and I'm ready to fly."

"When are you home?"

"Some time tomorrow. Not sure when."

"Okay," she said.

"You got back all right?"

"I got back, Ed, but I'm not sure about the all right."

"What do you mean?"

"I don't like it here."

"Here? Where's here?"

"Work."

"You having a trapeze artist moment?"

"That's only at the weekend, Ed. You know that. No, it's Monday, and if it's Monday it's something else, but I haven't decided what."

"Okay."

There was a silence. I heard the sound of phones ringing and doors squeaking.

"Ed?"

"Yeah?"

"We have to talk, Ed."

"Of course."

"When you get back."

"Sure."

"Okay." I heard the sound of another phone ringing. "I have to take that. Call me."

"I will," I said, and then she was gone.

THREE

EVERYONE AND EVERY PLACE IS THE SAME

I haven't been to as many places or seen as many things as David Attenborough has, but if I was repairing a wall in his back garden and he came out with a coffee and a couple of ginger nuts and we sat and chatted for ten minutes, I bet he'd agree with me if I said it doesn't matter if you're in Bermondsey, Ibiza, Amsterdam or Orkney – wherever you go or wherever you are, people are the same. Or if not the same, then very similar. For example: there was an old couple I met in Amsterdam who lived on a houseboat and she baked cakes and he made silver jewellery, and if you compared them to Elise and Alec of Stromness you'd say they were twins in every thing they did and said. And there was a nurse who worked in the Cancer Centre at Guys who looked and made love exactly like a barmaid I met in a club in Ibiza. And when I was in Margate once I had a pint with a bloke who was the spit of the guy who works behind the counter at a builders' merchants in Deptford, and they both had the same things to say about vegetarians. But it's not just the looks and sounds and sex and scents of people, or the fact that they do things for work that are similar, it's more than that. For everyone has the same hopes and worries, and everyone wants the same things. They want something good to eat, and something to drink. They crave comfort and warmth, someone to talk to, someone to love, someone who thinks about them every once in a while. Maybe a book to read or music to listen to, and the chance to go out and have some fun. And most people want to have work to do, and have the chance to find a meaning to their life. No one wants to reach the end of their life and think they haven't left a mark on the world, or made a difference to someone else's life. I say this but I know some people don't care. Some people say life can hang itself, for what's the point? Whatever I do and wherever I live it's going to be the same, so I might as well put two fingers up at the world and do what I want. Look at the world – places might change but the mind remains the same. It's obvious, I know, but sometimes it's difficult to see the obvious and easy to ignore what's under your nose. It's on your plate, but that doesn't mean you know where the knife and fork is.

Why do I think this stuff? I think this stuff because I can. I think this stuff because it's my birthday next week and I'll be thirty. I think this stuff because when I was in Orkney I met a couple of people who said they'd found paradise, and I've met people in Ibiza and Amsterdam who said the same, and last month I watched a programme about a bloke who'd jacked in his job in the city and bought a van and travelled to Argentina and found paradise there. And a couple of years ago Dad and I were asked to do a job for someone who then sold up and moved to Brighton, and she said it was paradise after Bermondsey, but eighteen months later I saw her again, and she'd moved back and was living in a flat on Tanner Street, and she said it was paradise because she was ten minutes from her work.

And the point? This is the point. Paradise lives in our heads so it can be anywhere and with anyone. One person's head is a unique head, so one person's paradise is someone else's nonsense. We find our place in the world and we move on. We say hello to someone and then we say goodbye to them. Life is just one long goodbye.

THREE CALLS RUNNING

When I was back in London my head went into a dive, hit the bottom of the pool and stayed there for a few days. I'd never felt anything like it. It took me a day to recover from the drive and then I went down with a cold. I don't know where I caught it, but it was a stinker. My nose ached and ran and I found myself in a dark place. I went to bed and stayed there for a couple of days. I'd never stayed in bed for a couple of days before, but as I lay in that pit and stared at the ceiling I was overcome with poor feelings. I didn't like it that I couldn't hear harbour water lapping below the window, and I didn't like it that there weren't any stones to go and look at. At school we were once told that a circle of stones used to stand at The Angel Islington, and virgins and sheep were taken there and sacrificed to a horned God with coaled eyes, but the stones are gone now so there'd be no point trying to find them. If I wanted to see old stones without driving miles I'd have to go to Stonehenge but I wasn't going to do that. Stonehenge is a toilet.

My mood wasn't helped when I tried to phone Claire and she didn't pick up three calls running, and when she did she went "Oh, hello…" like she didn't really want to talk to me. And when she said "Look…" I knew what she wanted to tell me. And when she said "I've got to go to Frankfurt for a couple of days. Can we talk when we get back?" there was nothing I could say. I know what "can we talk…" means.

"I'll be back on Thursday."

"Okay."

"I'll call you Friday."

I sneezed. "Great."

I wanted her to ask me if I was okay but she said "Sorry, Ed. I've got to run."

"Sure," I said, and she did and I lay back down and sneezed again.

I went back to work on Thursday. We started on an extension to a house between the Bricklayer's Arms and the Elephant. It was quite a big job. We had to bash out a wall between a kitchen and a conservatory, put in an RSJ, stick new French windows in the outside wall and a skylight in the roof. We'd been working for less than an hour when I dropped a lump hammer on my foot – no damage done, I was wearing steel caps – but after lunch I was whacking the wall and a splinter of brick flew into my face and cut me over the eye. It didn't look too bad but there was enough blood to fill a mug, so Dad took me to Guys, sat me in Urgent Care and said "I don't know what's the matter with you".

"I've had a cold."

"You've had colds before, Ed. They haven't made you careless."

"I know that."

He told me not to touch anything or anyone and went back to the job. I sat for half an hour and then a nurse came over and took me to a cubicle. Her name was Catalina, and I think she was Spanish. Her eyes were the colour of a good ganache, and she had plump lips. She smelt of roses and disinfectant. I sat on the side of a trolley and she looked at my wound and tutted and cleaned me up and put on some of those little plasters that hold a cut together. She was very efficient. When she was putting the plasters on, her neck was about six inches from my mouth. She had a mole underneath her chin. I stared at it. It was very beautiful. I like moles. Then she said "All done, Mr Beech."

"Thank you, Catalina. I owe you."

"You owe me nothing," she said. "This is my job."

"I know. But…"

"When was your last tetanus shot?"

"Last year."

"Okay," she said, "then you can go now."

I got off the trolley and put on my jacket. I know that once I would have said something more, maybe something about Spain or her hair or her touch, but I didn't. I thanked her again and she opened the curtain and I stepped out of the cubicle. She went back to her station and I went to the pub.

BACK IN THE MILLER

I suppose I thought I might see Magda and it might be awkward, but it was early and quiet, and I reckoned she'd probably be at work, and anyway I'd be able to handle whatever came up. I had a few words with Jim the landlord, bought a pint and found a corner table. A couple of people I knew came in and nodded in my direction but they left me alone. You know how it is – they knew I wanted to drink alone and respected that. We'd catch up another day. I drank and looked at the menu, but I didn't fancy anything. I thought I'd go to The Garrison so I called Mum, told her I wouldn't be in for tea, and then I called Marcus. He picked up on the second ring and said "Ed. Been meaning to call you."

I said "I've got your key."

"What key?"

"To Shore View. Stromness."

"Cool. Where are you?"

"The Miller. But I'm thinking of moving to The Garrison."

"Great minds. See you in an hour?"

"I'll be there," I said, and he hung up.

I left The Miller, crossed Guy Street Park and headed to Leathermarket Street. There was a house there with an artwork screwed to one of its outside walls. The art was made of words that had been cast in something like Perspex, but was probably something stronger. I'd passed it loads of times before and looked up at it but I'd never stopped to look properly. The words were by Charles Dickens who used to live round the corner. They read *"There are dark shadows on the earth, but its lights are stronger in the contrast. Some men, like bats or owls, have better eyes for the darkness than the light. We, who have no such optical powers, are better pleased to take our last parting look at the visionary companions of many solitary hours, when the brief sunshine of the world is blazing full upon them."*

The first time I read these words I didn't understand them, and reading them a few more times didn't help, but then, on that summer evening with the sound of laughing children playing in the park and music from balconies, and the chink of glasses from a bar, and the smell of something cooking drifting from an open window, they were crystal. I have solitary hours and I have a visionary companion, and when sunshine was blazing full upon her, I was very pleased. But now, I supposed, the sun had set or something. I didn't know.

The Garrison was at the far end of Leathermarket Street. It wasn't rammed but it was busy. I got a table by the window. I ordered a pint of FourPure and spent half an hour scrolling my phone and checking the menu. When Marcus arrived he greeted me like I was a long-lost friend, and clapped me on the shoulder and laughed and said "So you survived!"

"Just about."

He pointed at the cut over my eye. "You get that in Stromness?"

I shook my head. "This morning. I wasn't thinking."

"Looks nasty."

"I've had worse."

"I'll bet. What you drinking?"

"FourPure."

"You got it. Eating?"

"I think so."

"Cool. What you going for?"

"The roasted bass."

"I'll join you," he said, and went to the bar.

When he came back with the drinks he was shaking his head and said "Sometimes my sister's the limit."

"Claire?" I said, because I had to.

"That's the one."

"What's up?"

"Well, after the bowl fiasco – sorry about that, by the way…"

"Forget it."

"Now she's not sure if she wants to sell the house."

"Yeah?"

"Something about realising what she's been missing." He took a big swig of his beer. "How was she when she was up there?"

I shrugged. "Okay. Why?"

"She's been well weird since she got back."

"What do you mean?"

"She's normally pretty straight. Focused, you know. Her work's her life. At least I thought it was."

"I think she was happy to be up there," I said, and I told him that we'd been to the Ring of Brodgar and seen Hermann on Eday and eaten fish and chips by the harbour but that was all I told him. If he knew anything or suspected something he didn't say, and when he asked me what I thought of the place I said "It's different".

"That's for sure," he said, and then the food arrived and he said "Fabulous…" and tucked in. I took a deep breath and cut into my bass and said "Before I forget…" and I fished in my pocket for the front door key of the house in Stromness, and put it on the table.

"Cheers," he said, and he picked it up. "And let me know what I owe you."

"Sure," I said. "Invoice to the Jam Factory?"

"If you want. Or just tell me and I'll give you the notes."

"That'd be useful."

"So tell me," he said, and I did and he pulled out his wallet and counted out the notes and added a ton on top and I thanked him and he thanked me and we tapped our glasses together and that was where we left it in The Garrison on that day in July 2017 with the heat of the day dripping from the walls of the pub, and the little gang of smokers laughing by the door, and the last bike messenger of the day spinning down the street. And when my phone buzzed in my pocket and I took it out and there was a text from Claire, I said nothing. I just stared at the words and felt my heart in my chest and I thought that what I needed then was a whisky to go with the pint, and then another.

A NICE FLAT BUT THERE'S NO WAY I COULD LIVE THERE

Claire's place was a new build in a smart block half a mile from Cutty Sark. It was a two bed (one en-suite) with a good sized living area. I didn't rate the flooring (average laminate throughout) but as far as I could see, it didn't need any work doing. There was a great view of Canary Wharf from the Juliet, and although there was plenty of traffic on the river, the sound insulation was good.

There were a couple of her dad's pictures on the wall, books and ornaments on floating shelves, and deep rugs. Lucie Rie's bowl lived in a glass cabinet that stood in the corner of the main bedroom, and Hermann's sculpture stood on her dressing table.

The kitchen was a useful size. There were some top appliances. I did more cooking when I lived in that flat than I'd ever done. I learned to make a decent soufflé, and a good haddock and corn chowder with Jewish crackers on top. Claire would come home from work and watch me. We didn't argue but sometimes she had words with me, like when I told her I'd had to knock off early to take Barney to the vet. "Nothing serious," I said. "He had an ear infection."

"Poor Barney," she said.

"Well, if he will listen to Barry Manilow."

"Stop it."

"No. He borrows Mum's CDs. Puts them in the van's player when we're not looking. I'm not kidding."

"Barry Manilow?"

"Yeah. And that other guy."

"What other guy?"

"Bach."

"No, Ed," she said, and she held up her finger. "You have to stop that."

"Stop what? You cross 'em, I'll nod 'em in."

She looked at me for a moment and shook her head. "Your crap jokes, Ed. Actually, they're not even jokes. They're just rubbish."

"I'm sorry."

"You should be."

"I am."

"No you're not."

And another time she came home from work and she was steaming and cursing, and I had sit her down and she told me that this bloke from America had been in the office and called her a "dumb broad" and she'd reported him to HR but they're said "you'll be lucky, Claire. He's a partner…"

And the next day he said something about everyone in the London office being slow and stupid, and if he had his way he'd close it, and that was it for Claire, and she told them they could stuff their trade-related credit insurance up their global solutions because she was moving to Italy to grow grapes. Except she wasn't. She couldn't drink then, so she didn't want to think about wine. No. She was moving to Ireland to breed horses. Or she was going to buy Marcus's share of the house in Stromness, turn the stone shed into a workshop and make stained glass windows, violins or orreries.

"What are orreries?"

"Models of the solar system."

"Oh."

"Are they to scale?"

"Of course they're not."

"Why not?"

"Because if they were, and the sun was, say the size of an orange, then Pluto would be the size of a grain of sand and over a thousand miles away. Orreries just show relative motion, and even then they're not that accurate. They're just pretty."

"Okay."

"So. Want to come with me?"

"Where?"

"Stromness."

She put her hand on her belly. "It'll be a great place to have the baby. Better than round here."

I had to think about it. "I don't know," I said. "I'd have to think about it."

"Okay."

"And speak to Dad. We've got a business."

"I know."

"And Mum."

"Of course."

"You know I've never lived anywhere else but here. And Orkney – it's a long way."

"Look," she said, and pointed out of the window at a plane. It had just left London City, and was turning north. "An hour and a half to Aberdeen. Grab some lunch, pick up a Toblerone and you're in Kirkwall forty minutes later. Half an hour in the car and you're in the door. Four hours, tops. You could leave here after breakfast and be in Stromness in time for your afternoon nap."

"Were you ever in sales?"

"Yes."

"Where?"

"My first Saturday job. M&S. Lingerie. The pants I could sell. I was a natural."

"I bet you were."

"I was."

The week before, Dad had been talking about how the weekend in Margate had made him think that he and Mum should be slowing down. "We're not getting any younger," he'd said, and "this game is starting to play merry hell with my back."

I said to Claire "What would I do?"

"When? Where?"

"In Stromness."

"I don't know. Painting and decorating? What do you think? Or maybe something you're really good at."

"Steady…"

"Oh you know, Ed. Come on."

"What?"

"That place could do with another restaurant. You do the chefing, I'll do the wine. We work from April to October, maybe do some business over Christmas, spend the rest of the year doing not a lot."

"You've got this worked out, haven't you?"

"Pretty much. You got any savings?"

"A few grand. You?"

"Some."

"Meaning loads."

She shrugged. "I never spent a lot."

"What would you do with this place?"

"Let it. It'll pay the rent on the restaurant, and some."

"You have been thinking about it."

"I'm always thinking."

"I know. Any others?"

"Other whats?"

"Thoughts."

"Other than the usual?"

"You have usual thoughts?"

"And that means?"

"What can I tell you, Claire?"

"Tell me whatever you want, Edward Beech."

WE ARE THE
STROMNESS DINNER

I used to live in Bermondsey, which is an area of London. When I was younger I used to go with anything that moved but then I met Claire. I didn't think she'd look at me twice but I did some work for her and we got on. Then we did more than that on a beach and then we slept together.

She was a dream. The day after we slept together she said she could smell things she hadn't smelt before, things like marzipan and almonds, but it wasn't that she could, it was because she was pregnant and her senses were blazing.

She had her own place. I lived at home. She asked me if I wanted to move in with her. I said yes. She said great. I was there for a few months.

I was there for a few months and thinking the months might turn into years but then things changed at her work and we talked. To begin with we just chatted and then it got serious and we made some decisions. These decisions turned into plans and the plans became actions. She left her work and I told my Dad I was going to do something else. Then we moved into her father's old house in Stromness, rented an old shop on Alfred Street and turned it into a restaurant. It wasn't as quick and easy as that, but it was close.

We did think about calling the place The Bowl but we don't like being obvious. Obvious is too easy, and we don't like easy. Then we thought we'd call it The Stromness Diner but it's not American and we thought people would think it was actually The

275

Stromness Dinner so that's what we called it. If people need it spelt out for them there's a sign over the window.

Two months after we moved Claire had our baby. We called her Eve, which was Claire's mother's name. She's a good baby with a good pair of lungs and big feet. She started smiling at six weeks and ate a piece of melon when she was four months. The nurse said she was bonny.

When I'm working I'll cook fish, veggie, meat and pasta but I don't do stir-fries. If we want fresh fish we fetch it from Orkney Fish, and if we want meat we go to Flett's on John Street. We get all our wine from Kirkness & Gorie in Kirkwall. The bloke in there knows loads about it. He also does cheese. One of my specials is hasenpfeffer. We've got seventeen reviews on tripadvisor.co.uk and only one person said we were crap and she didn't even eat here.

We're busy. Last week we were open five days and did 160 covers on seven tables. We stole a waitress from one of the hotels in town. Her name is Sandra. She's excellent. We all like to work.

Claire is full and beautiful. She has long fingers and doesn't wear gold. I love her face and I love the way she says "Do something about the front door, Ed. It's sticking." She does the accounts and knows about wine. I like wine too, but in a different way to the way she likes it. She likes it because she likes to look at it in the glass, judge its smell, taste it and ponder the aftertaste. She'll say things like "I'm getting terracotta flower pots warming on a Tuscan terrace..." and I'll say "I'm getting a lot of grape." I can't help myself. I should also say that I'm bigger than Claire. People know I'm in the kitchen. I try not to clatter but I do sometimes. I stay around fifteen stone. That's a healthy weight for my size, though I could do with loosing a few pounds.

I like chefing and I keep the kitchen neat. It has to be. If it's not, things get chaotic. I keep my uniform neat. No one wants to see a splattered chef, so I wear a proper jacket and an apron, and good shoes. Claire says my neatness is a joy and my plates are neat too – I won't have careless arrangements or splashes. Customers like it when everything's perfect about their meal, and I do too.

Our Eve doesn't do a lot at the moment. She likes food but I don't know where she puts it. She's a bit round in places, but otherwise I don't think anyone would tell her to cut down on pureed sweet potato.

We did think about getting a dog but the house is small so we got a cat. She's black with white paws so we called her Mittens. She looks like she couldn't catch a fly, and she can't. She'll ignore it, you and anything else you've got to offer. She's the most aloof cat in Stromness. People try to get friendly with Mittens but she ignores them. She likes poached salmon and dozing on walls.

So this is us and we are the Stromness Dinner. Many types of dishes prepared, not just dinner. No meal too small. Tables for families, tables for two, tables for single people who want to sit in the corner and read a book while they eat. There's a good wine list.

All the tables have a view of the water, the boats and the Scrabster ferry. I know the timetable so I know when it's coming in and know when it's leaving, so I try to avoid seeing it. It's a big ship.